"Doesn't mean we cannot come to agreement for passage over Wind River. Gold is always good."

"I've no gold," I said.

"Silver then."

"None."

"Any coin?"

I shook my head. "Sadly, no."

The horse looked at my throat. "What about necklace?"

It was pewter. Not worth much, but it had sentimental value. It was a gift from my pixie father on my last birthday. I thought about it, and I could hear old Thunderrod in my mind's ear telling me he could always buy me another so long as I survived.

"Deal. I'll give it to you once I'm safely on the other side," I said.

"No, too easy for you to run off, and then where will poor Aughisky be? Necklace first before passage."

I took it off and held it dangling by its chain. "Necklace for safe passage."

The water horse reached out with his mouth and plucked the necklace from my fingers with his lips. I had to force myself not to pull back. "Necklace for passage is what I said."

An arrow whizzed by my head, clipping my ear and Aughisky's mane. I turned to see Oaf lean out from behind a tree, notching another arrow. The wind probably just saved my life.

"Who be shooting at Aughisky?"

"One of Thandau's graycoats, and he's lining up his next shot. Time for running and swimming," I said.

"Aughisky thinks little wing girl is right. Get on!"

I did, and no sooner had I sat upon his back then we were off running down the shore. I barely got a hold of his mane before I looked back to see an arrow sticking out of the ground where we had stood.

Aughisky ran so fast and far that in moments, I could no longer see Oaf.

"Think Aughisky lost graycoat."

"Looks that way," I said.

"Foolish soldier, try to kill Aughisky. Not realize he on wrong side of food chain." Before I could say anything, he ran into the water. A rapid hit me hard enough to knock me over, but I didn't budge. I tried to move, but my lower limbs were caught fast.

"Aughisky, my legs –"

"Yes, Aughisky knows. Aughisky has special power, won't let rider get off."

I didn't like the way he said "get" instead of "fall", but before I could question this, he dove beneath the water. I barely had time to get a breath before we sank to the bottom of the river where Aughisky ran as easily as he had along the shore.

The horse could breathe underwater but I couldn't. I tried to get off, but Aughisky had told the truth about his sticking power.

Drowning is not a good way to die. I didn't survive the damn graycoats to get killed by a swimming horse.

BOOKS BY PATRICK THOMAS

<u>**The Murphy's Lore™ series**</u>
TALES FROM BULFINCHE'S PUB
FOOLS' DAY
THROUGH THE DRINKING GLASS
SHADOW OF THE WOLF
REDEMPTION ROAD
BARTENDER OF THE GODS

<u>**Murphy's Lore After Hours™**</u>
NIGHTCAPS
EMPTY GRAVES
THE MUG LIFE

<u>**Murphy's Lore Startenders™**</u>
STARTENDERS
CONSTELLATION PRIZE

<u>**Murphy's Lore After Hours™ Universe**</u>
<u>**Terrorbelle:**</u>
FAIRY WITH A GUN
FAIRY RIDES THE LIGHTNING
TERRORBELLE THE UNCONQUERED
<u>**Agent Karver:**</u>
RITES OF PASSAGE *(with John French)*
DEAD TO RITES
<u>**Hell's Detective:**</u>
LORE & DYSORDER
BULLETS & BRIMSTONE
(with John French)
THE CASE OF THE MOON MANIAC
(graphic novel with Blair Webb)
<u>**Hexcraft:**</u>
BY DARKNESS CURSED
BY INVOCATION ONLY
<u>**Soul for Hire:**</u>
GREATEST HITS

<u>**Xiles:**</u>
EXILE & ENTRANCE

<u>**Dear Cthulhu™ Series**</u>
HAVE A DARK DAY
GOOD ADVICE FOR BAD PEOPLE
CTHULHU KNOWS BEST
WHAT WOULD CTHULHU DO?
CTHULHU HAPPENS
CTHULHU EXPLAINS IT ALL

<u>**Mystic Investigators™ series**</u>
MYSTIC INVESTIGATORS
MEAN STREETS
ONCE MORE IN CRIME omnibus
by Patrick Thomas & Diane Raetz
SHADOWS & BRIMSTONES omnibus
by Patrick Thomas & John L. French

<u>**Playworlds:**</u>
AS THE GEARS TURN:
Tales of Steamworld

<u>**YA:**</u>
THE WILDSIDHE CHRONICLES
OMNIBUS *(contributing author)*

<u>**Anthologies as co-editor**</u>
NEW BLOOD *(with Diane Raetz)*
CAMELOT 13 *(with John French)*

<u>**THE JACK GARDNER MYSTERIES**</u>
THE ASSASSAINS' BALL *(with John French)*

<u>**Writing as Patrick T. Fibbs**</u>
UNDEAD KID DIARIES™:
OVER MY DEAD BODY
BABE B. BEAR MYSTERIES™:
BAD HAIR DAY
5 SILLY MONSTERS JUMPING O
THE ZED: *an Ughaboos™ picture book*

TERRORBELLE THE UNCONQUERED

Tales From Terrorbelle's Early Years

PATRICK THOMAS

PADWOLF PUBLISHING INC.
WWW.PADWOLF.COM
www.facebook.com/Padwolf

WWW.PATTHOMAS.NET
www.facebook.com/PatrickThomasAuthor
WWW.PATTHOMAS.NET

TERRORBELLE THE UNCONQUERED
© 2019 Patrick Thomas

COVER ART BY DANIEL R. HORNE
COVER LAYOUT BY ROY MAURITSEN
BOOK EDITED BY JOHN L. FRENCH

LOOKING A GIFT HORSE was originally published in *Bad-Ass Faeries: It's Elemental* edited by Danielle Ackley-McPhail, L. Jagi Lamplighter, Lee Hillman, and Jeff Lyman
BENEATH DARKNESS was originally published in *Warfear, A Collection of Strange War Tales* edited by Leslie Ellis
BENEATH THE SEA OF TEARS was originally published in *Sails & Sorcery: Tales of Nautical Fantasy* edited by W. H. Horner
THE LESSER was originally published in *Demons: A Clash of Steel Anthology* edited by Jason M Waltz
LUCKY DAYE was originally published in *Nightcaps*
VIRGIN TERRITORY was originally published in *Hear Them Roar* edited by CJ Henderson and Patrick Thomas

ISBN: 13 digit 978-1-890096-85-4   10 digit 1-890096-85-7
Printed in the USA First Printing

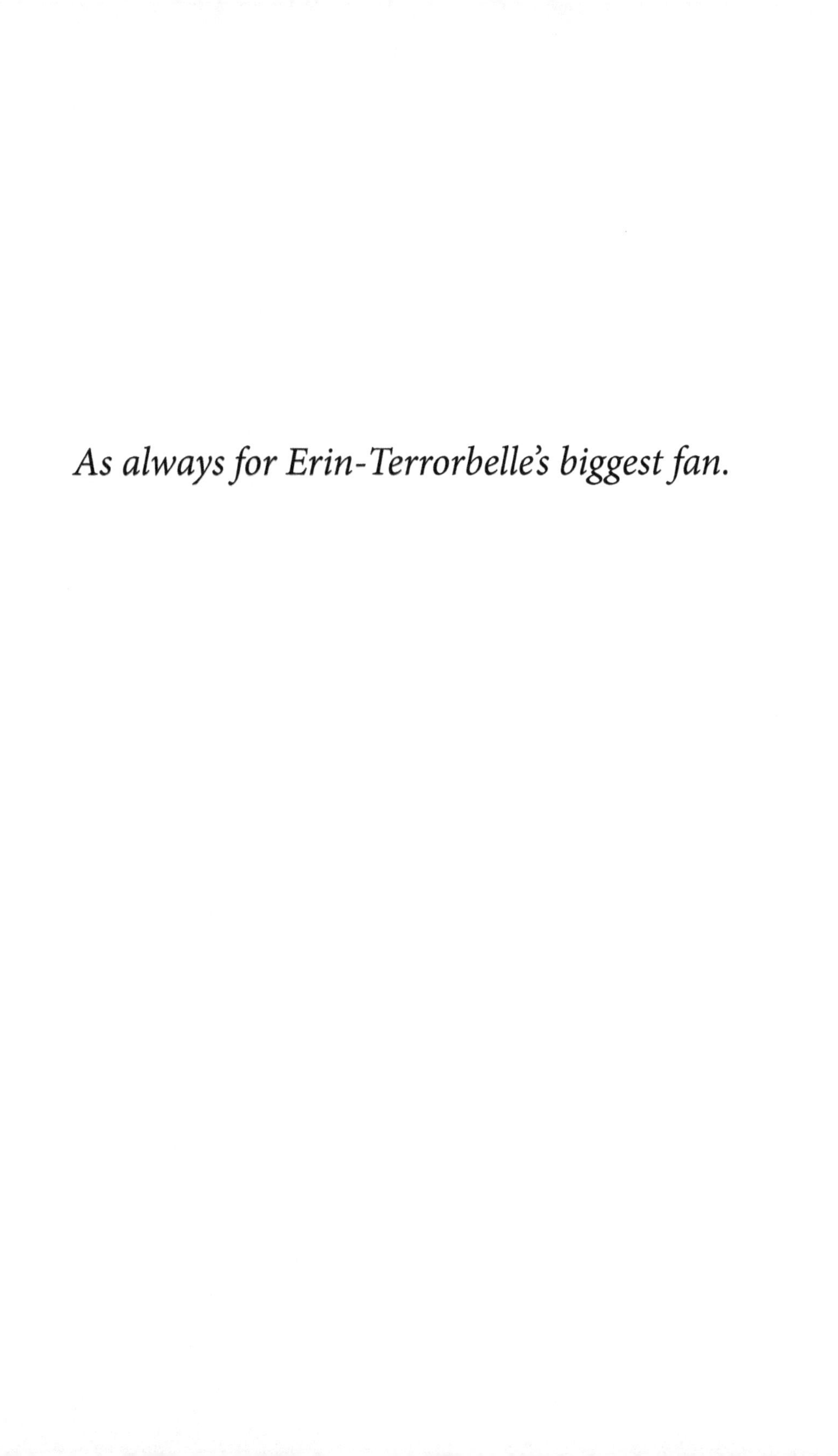

As always for Erin-Terrorbelle's biggest fan.

CONTENTS

Bonus Swords of the Daemor tales!

THE ZOMBIE OF OGRE ROCK

I'm not one to waste time wondering about what-ifs, with one exception: What would my life have been like if my mother had taken me on a different path on the day that ended my innocence? Would it have changed things, or did the fates just have it in for us? Would Thandau's soldiers have come after us no matter which way we went? I find a small comfort in believing that somewhere in some other universe there's a little Terrorbelle who had a happy childhood untouched by the savagery of war. I like to ponder about the woman she grew to be.

In none of my imaginings does she become a soldier like I did. She doesn't have to. In her life, there's no need for revenge or to quiet the evil soldiers that haunt her dreams. She never wakes up screaming in the night from what happened that day.

The Terrorbelle that is me isn't so lucky. That day, more than anything else, is what shaped me into who I am today. I don't think anyone else can ever understand how truly disturbing I find that.

I was a child, the Faerie equivalent of an eleven-year-old. I was very big for my age. And very small. It depended on which side of my family was sizing me up. Dad is a pixie, Mom was an ogre. I towered over one side and was underfoot with the others, managing to be both without being either. It's the curse of a half-breed. By the standards of both, I'm not terribly good looking. I have a pixie shape, but with ogre proportions. Pixies are painfully pretty, while ogres pride themselves on ugliness. I was neither. The blood of each affected the other, most notably in my wings. Instead of delicate, they're razor sharp. And they worked, at least in Faerie, although I couldn't fly overly far without resting because of my size.

Dad wasn't the type to settle down, so I stayed mostly with my Mom. Flying was an issue with her for lots of reasons. Mostly, it was because ogres didn't fly. They threw rocks at things that did, trying to knock them out of the sky, often eating them once they hit the ground. She thought it was too dangerous for me to use my wings but stopped short of forbidding me.

On this particular day, we were going to visit my grandmother. Ogres show affection very physically, usually by smashing each other. As they are very durable and hard to hurt, it's not usually a bad thing. I was tough, but not so much that I enjoyed being hit. My grandmother was known to be very affectionate, so much so, in fact, that those she gave love taps were often seen soaring through the air around Ogre Rock.

Gran realized I wasn't as sturdy as the rest of the family and never hit me. Even better, if she ever heard about anyone ever mistreating me, she made sure it never happened again. I adored her and insisted on visiting her often. Mom usually indulged me. I could have gotten there faster by flying, but since Mom was ground-bound, I walked with her.

"The weather's nice," I said.

"Urgh." Which loosely translated as "I guess." Ogres tend toward the strong, silent type. My mother was no exception. "Too sunny."

Mom's skin was relatively pale. After twelve or so hours in strong sunlight, it turned the slightest shade of pink. She preferred foggy days, finding them more relaxing. Mist helped keep her hidden from food and thrill hunters. Some folks believed ogres to be a threat. In truth, the ogre reputation for eating flesh is somewhat exaggerated. It's not that ogres won't eat other kinds of people, or each other, for that matter—meat is meat after all—but most prefer to avoid sentients. Making a meal of a person caused too many headaches, particularly when their kin came seeking revenge.

Those who sought out food that could engage in pre-dinner conversation were only a small part of the population and were considered deviants among their fellow ogres. Problems arose because other races didn't care to make distinctions. One on one, ogres are as strong as any race in Faerie short of giants or dragons, but anyone can be hunted and killed by a well-organized group. Ogre hunting was considered good sport by some. After all, they were all cannibalistic scum, so who cared if the occasional one was slaughtered for fun?

"I like sunny days," I said.

Mom's grunt, this time, was her equivalent of a laugh. "You would. Me blame father." Mom could speak using good grammar. She just didn't care to.

"Dad's not so bad."

"Me know. That why me not squish him." Dad was big for a pixie, but Mom was bigger than most of the male ogres. Dad's got a real way with the ladies. "Plus, he good to our little girl." Mom mussed my hair, almost knocking me over.

Which is when nets fell over each of us. I froze, terrified. Mom roared and tried to tear the ties, but they were too strong. Instead, she reached a single hand through a gap and grabbed my net to pull it tighter.

"Buzz wings fast," Mom ordered. With her holding the ropes, my razor sharp wings sliced through the ropes. The vestiges of my pixie heritage were dangerous weapons and could make up for my strength difference with the more aggressive predators and ogre relations.

I moved to free Mom as soldiers came out of the underbrush.

"Fly, my little Terror," she said.

"I'm not leaving you," I screamed.

"Me your mother and…" Mom stopped. She knew ordering me to do something was the easiest way to make sure I did the opposite. "There are only seven of them. Mama can handle them."

I stood wavering, and the soldiers crept closer, holding long spears. Best not to get too close to an ogre if you want all your limbs to remain attached.

"Go!" At the shout, I took off into the air. I knew it was bad when she whispered after me, "Mama loves you, my little Terror."

I hovered close enough to see what was happening, but far enough away that arrows wouldn't reach me.

"What about that one, gon?" said a soldier. Gon is equivalent to the rank of a sergeant in Faerie.

"Let it go. We were told to gather ogres and it's not one. This one will do fine."

The soldiers were talking about my mother like she was a head of cabbage they were told to buy at market. But cabbage doesn't fight anything like an ogre. Few things do.

Even under a net, Mom didn't go down easily. The first soldier who came close had his right arm snapped. They were more cautious after that, beating her with long clubs while fighting to shackle her wrists and ankles. The cost to the soldiers wasn't low, but they outnumbered her, and the shackles were enspelled, limiting her strength. Once all four limbs were bound, the chain magiks made her weak as a babe.

Still, she fought, not willing to give an inch, but now her blows may as well have been hits with a puffy dandelion for all the damage they were doing. With Mother subdued, the soldiers turned toward me and started firing arrows. They were coming too close, so I pretended to fly away.

What happened next is something I still have trouble talking about to this day. Those soldier bastards had my mother at their mercy and showed none. They stripped her down and began to force themselves on her.

I broke a limb off a tree and dived at them. I was strong, but

I was still a child. I managed to brain the one who was atop my mother, but the others grabbed hold of me. I had been taught for so long to not use my wings to hurt others that I hesitated instead of slicing the soldiers to ribbons. They were soldiers, and even with my untrained struggles, it didn't take them long to immobilize me in shackles identical to those that held my mother. They conformed to the size of the limb they were put on. The spell made me so weak I could barely lift my arms with the chains, let alone fight back.

I was made to watch as they all took turns with my mother, then they turned their attentions to me. Despite the shackles, my mother surged up at the nearest soldier, intent on rending him limb from limb, but the magic that made her weak also made her slow. The soldier hit her in the middle of the forehead with something that looked like a branding stick. Eldritch energies, darker than the blackest night, leapt out into Mama, making her convulse and twitch. The soldier then slit her throat, her blood spraying all over, including on me.

"Mama!"

My screams weren't enough to bring my mother back from the dead, but they made the soldiers laugh. And they were still laughing when they turned back to me. My clothes were torn off me, and each of them had their turn with me. Two forced themselves on me multiple times. My pleading and begging for them to stop only seemed to encourage them, so I closed my eyes and bit my lip bloody, unwilling to give them the satisfaction of having me scream again. One of them stood at my head, forcing my eyelids open.

Finally, they were done, and I was no longer being held down by hands. I crawled to the corpse of my mother and tried to cuddle up into her dead arms, praying to anyone who could hear to make everything that had just happened be only a dream.

My only answer was more laughter from the bastard

soldiers.

"She wants her Mama to hug her and make things all better," a soldier mocked.

The soldier with the branding stick pointed it at Mama's body. "She gave us a good time, so I guess we can help her out. *Spaisdeireachd.*"

I couldn't understand why he shouted out for her to walk until I felt her arms wrap around me. "Mama?"

"Your Mama belongs to us now," the soldier with the brand said.

"And Thandau," said another. The first glared like he wanted to hit the second, but held his tongue and his blows.

"Ogre, bring the girl and follow us," the one with the brand ordered as he snapped and the shackles fell off my mother.

My mother stood and obeyed.

"Mama, what are you doing? Let go of me, please," I pleaded. Mama didn't respond which only made the soldiers laugh more. We walked right onto a Faerie path, the world around us shimmered and glowed as time and space bent around us, transporting us to a clearing that could have been a stone's throw or half a world away. Unless you know about a path, it's smart to avoid it. You never know where you'll end up or if you'd be able to get home.

We emerged in a heavily armed camp filled with graycoats, Thandau's soldiers. The soldiers who had brutalized us passed us along to another soldier.

"Good job on the ogre, but what am I supposed to do with this other one? Thandau only wants ogres for his zombie battalion."

"Lokhagos," (the Faerie equivalent of a captain) "you can add her to the slave pens or cut her throat. Makes no difference to me. Although…" The soldier who had held the brand ordered my mother to put me down, then he leaned in and whispered something I couldn't hear. I was still without clothes.

My mother's arms had been strategically placed to cover me, but as I stood there, I felt incredibly vulnerable. The soldier who seemed in charge of the camp smiled and stared at me, managing to make me feel violated with just a look.

"I suppose the lads could do with a spot of entertainment later." I shuddered as another soldier dragged me to a cage and shoved me inside. The door was slammed behind me. I watched as the soldiers who had attacked us disappeared back along the Faerie path, and I admit I was glad to see them go.

My mother stood in the same spot, unmoving. There were five other ogres stationed around the camp, each seemingly in the same undead condition as my mother. When I thought the soldiers weren't looking, I tried to get my mother's attention, but she didn't so much as twitch.

Hours later, a soldier came over to the cage and slipped a bucket of water with a rag through a space in the bars.

"Wash up," he ordered, and walked away. I had never felt dirtier in my life, so I complied. It didn't help. Not long after I was done, the soldier returned and grabbed my chain, yanking me out and practically dragging me to the middle of the camp. Night had fallen, and a huge fire was burning. Twenty soldiers had gathered there. I was tossed in the center of the congregation. I held the rag in front of my groin and my wings were folded over to cover my chest.

The soldier in charge came up and pulled the rag out of my hands. "No need to cover up, girl. You're among friends here. Dance for us." The lokhagos started stripping out of his armor, making it clear he was planning on violating me with more than a look this time. Other soldiers were following suit. I tried to flap my wings and fly away, but the magic of the shackles kept me land-locked.

The lokhagos grabbed me by the wrist. "There'll be none of that." Then he yelled because I had managed to slice his arm with my wings. After the gang rape, I no longer cared if I hurt him or anybody else. He smacked my face, knocking me to the ground. "You'll pay for that, you little ckuffer."

He ordered men to pin my arms, with my wings between me and the ground. For me to use them again meant I'd cut myself more than I would them.

As he tried to force my knees apart, I screamed for my mother. Begging and pleading for her to save me. Some Daemor might be ashamed of admitting that weakness, but I was not yet a soldier, never mind a Daemor. I was only a frightened little girl who still thought her Mama could make things better. I had already learned that life didn't always work that way.

But sometimes it did.

Somewhere behind the line of soldiers waiting for their turn with me, there was a sound like a melon being splattered. It was soon followed by two more, and then the sound of soldiers screaming as the corpse of my mother moved to crush their skulls between her fingers.

Soldiers stabbed at her, but Mama's corpse didn't even try to block the blows. She didn't need to. Any harm the weapons did to her started to heal the moment the weapon was pulled back. The soldier on top of me leapt off and watched as my zombie Mama ripped both of a soldier's arms off his body, then stomped him into a fleshy pudding before he could bleed to death.

The lokhagos pulled his trousers on with one hand. With the other, he grabbed a medallion on a chain around his neck that bore the same mark that had been branded onto my mother's forehead.

"Stop. I command you."

Mama stopped an arm's reach away from the lokhagos.

"You are supposed to be an obedient corpse. How did you manage to do this on your own?"

My dead Mama didn't answer.

"You will restrain this child and not harm another one of

my men. We will make her pay for your transgressions. Do you understand?"

Mama never said, but her answer was pretty clear as she reached out and crushed his head into jelly. As the soldier fell, Mama's hand reached for the medallion. Her fingers burst into flame when they made contact, but she didn't drop it. Instead, she handed it to me, then tore the shackles from my wrists and ankles.

Another soldier yelled at the other dead ogres to destroy her, and they moved to obey.

Mama was strong, maybe even stronger dead than when she was alive, but there was no way for her to fight five other ogres. It was my turn to save her. I raised the medallion up and said, "No. Stop the soldiers."

The zombie ogres moved to obey me, but they were only immobilizing the men. Mama reached out with her fingers and touched the medallion. Again her flesh became fiery. Although I didn't hear Mama speak, somehow she conveyed a message to the other dead ogres, and they proceeded to slaughter the soldiers. All but one. He managed to flee down the Faerie path and vanish. Not even zombies would chase him.

Part of me was horrified at the carnage, but a darker part reveled in it, because of what had been done to me and Mama, and what these men had been about to do. I shed no tears for them.

When there was nothing moving in the camp that didn't have at least some ogre blood, I hugged Mama. At first, nothing happened, but slowly her arms wrapped around me.

"I love you, Mama."

The sound that came out of her mouth sounded like something dying, but the words were comforting. "Mama... loves... Terror."

Before I could ask any more questions, troops came rushing off the path. There must have been a hundred.

Mama again touched the medallion, and the other dead ogres moved to attack the new soldiers.

Mama pulled a knife out of her chest and handled it to me.

"Terror fly… to Babbey." My granny.

"But…"

"No come back… this time. Mama… dead. Not want baby dead. Please go… Promise Mama."

"I won't…"

Mama lifted me up so our eyes were even. "Promise!" Her yell shook the leaves off nearby trees.

"I promise."

Just then, an arrow lodged itself in her chest, missing me by the span of a hand. Mama pulled her arms back and pitched me over the nearby treetops. It was a game we used to play when I was little and we were near Gran's. She'd toss me up and I'd fly down back into her arms and she'd do it again. Everyone was so scared of Gran that it was the only place Mom felt safe letting me fly.

I could hear the sounds of battle below, but this time I didn't look back. If I did, I'd never leave, and I had promised Mama.

I pushed the thought of what was happening to her out of my mind, filling my thoughts instead with the men who had raped us, then killed Mama and turned her into that thing.

I suppose I owed the bastard who held my eyes open a debt. Unable to look away, I had no choice but to let the faces of each of my attackers burn themselves into my memory. It would make hunting them down and killing them that much easier.

Looking A Gift Horse

Branches slapping your face hurt. It doesn't matter if you're on the ground or fifty feet off it. Flying through a forest is a particularly stupid thing to do, even if you have the option of blaming it on the fact that you're an eleven-year-old girl on the run from one of the soldiers who killed your mother.

The scum was chasing me, but no one besides me would blame him for it. It seemed only reasonable since I started things by stalking him and his partner. I had a good motive. A great one really. Those bastards and their friends... They did horrible things to my mother and made me watch. They made my mother watch as they did them to me and then killed her. I was lucky enough to get away. If you call being alone in Faerie and unable to sleep without waking up screaming from nightmares lucky.

I coped. One thing helped me continue to survive – the thought of all of those soldiers dead.

Seems he wanted the same thing for me, but so far that hadn't worked out for him. Mama's little Terror doesn't die easy.

Didn't mean that the damn graycoat stopped trying to kill me. And having pink hair made it easier for him to follow me. It sort of stood out among all the greens and browns.

It was down to which of us got the other first. The smart wager would be on the trained soldier, not the scrap kid. Even now I heard Mama tell me not to call myself scrap, that my parents were two different races didn't matter, but with a mama who was an ogre and a daddy who's a pixie, it was an apt term.

I'd bet on me, even if I haven't proved myself very good at killing yet, which was entirely my fault. This whole mess started when I found the graycoat soldiers' camp…

It hadn't been easy, but a combination of determination and luck led me to them. The black-hearted killers had been sent out on an extended patrol, just the two of them. No other graycoats to worry about getting in the way. It seemed like such a good idea.

I didn't know the graycoats' real names, but I'll never forget their faces. I gave them names, rather than figure out what their mothers had called them. It seemed unlikely that they even had mothers. If they did, how could they kill someone else's?

I called them Oaf and Tiny. Tiny was tall. My term of scorn referred to something other than his height.

Oaf and Tiny slept, not worried or smart enough to have one of them keep watch.

Getting into their camp was child's play. I stood over the mother killers, watching as the light from their fire flickered across their faces.

Neither looked to be the embodiment of evil that I knew them to be. The knife I'd been given during my escape from the slavers felt heavy, but it was barely the length of my forearm. It sat in my palm, just waiting to slit their throats. True, my wings were scrap like me. The beauty of pixie and the hardness of ogre. One flap and I could likely cut the mother killers' heads off without the knife, but the idea of using the only beautiful parts of me to kill made me sick to my stomach. More sick than the thought of killing alone.

And if the truth be told, as I stood over their sleeping forms I discovered something: killing two sleeping men in cold blood—even two of Thandau's soldiers—wasn't something I could bring myself to do, even with everything they'd done.

Everything inside of me burned with the desire to see them dead for what they did to us. Yet killing for killing's sake was something that Mama had always taught me was wrong. I doubt the mother killers would appreciate the irony.

I couldn't bring myself to end them while they lay helpless.

So I got stupid. I kicked dirt in their faces to wake them up so I could kill them while they were conscious instead.

It was idiotic, a mistake of epic proportions. The soldiers snapped awake.

"What?" Tiny yelled as he grabbed his sword. The weapon was quite a bit longer than Oaf's. Babbey, my granny, would say he was trying to make up for something else. I missed the days when I only pretended to know what she meant.

Already alert, Oaf called out, "It's the winged scrap bitch. She got away!"

They had left me in a graycoat camp, a toy to be passed around among Thandau's soldiers.

"Damn right I got away from your slave camp. You won't be so lucky," I said. "I'm going to kill you for what you did to my mama."

Tiny leapt up and threw his bedroll aside as he held his sword in front of him. Oaf rose slowly and tossed his bedroll at me like it was a net. It covered my razor-sharp wings. He rushed at me, knocking me to the ground where he used his arms to pin my entangled shoulders and wings. I dropped my knife and struggled to reach it.

"Should have killed us while we were sleeping," Oaf said.

At that moment, I couldn't agree more. "If I'd known I'd had your permission, I'd have done it."

"Smart mouth. Not the scared little thing you were last time." Oaf reached back and smacked me across the face. "I don't like smart mouths, little scrap girl."

Tiny was giggling, as he hopped back from one foot to the other. "Go easy on her." I was shocked. None of the graycoats had shown the slightest inclination for mercy before. "She came to us. You know what that means, right? The scrap didn't get enough the first time and she wants more." Tiny dropped his pants and stepped toward me.

My nightmare had re-entered the waking world. Everything I could see turned red. Anger, not thought, controlled me as I smashed my forehead into Oaf's nose, making his world join mine in the red zone.

I got to my feet and struck Oaf with my elbow, then kicked him in a place I'd much rather be unfamiliar with. I may be scrap, but I was strong. The bastard fell to his side with only a brief pause on his knees.

I ripped the bedroll from me and tossed it away. Tiny came waddling at me with his sword, but having wings had its advantages. I flew up and over his head, flipping in the process to land behind him and pick up the knife I'd dropped.

Tiny spun with his blade aimed for my neck. I ducked as fast as I could, but his sword took a piece of my scalp and some of my pink hair as it whizzed by.

I stabbed forward with my knife. I'd like to say that the part of his male anatomy that I cut into was a target of convenience, but I can't for sure. All I know is it felt good, angry good, especially as Tiny let out a high-pitched scream as he became a eunuch. He swung his sword wildly back at me—his missing bits must have made him forget his soldier training—but I was too close. His forearm hit me in the side of the head, letting me grab hold of the hilt.

I bit his arm, pulled, and the sword was mine. I took a step back and pointed the blade at him the same way he'd done it to me. Tiny pulled a dagger from under his arm and lunged at me, but overstepped. He tripped, helped by the fact that he hadn't bothered to pull up his pants which still were wrapped around his ankles. I rammed the sword forward as he fell. His chest and the blade met. I think it is safe to say that the probably got the better of that meeting, at least judging by the look on Tiny's face as the blade went in one side of him and out the other.

Tiny fell over, sliding off my blade like well-cooked meat off a spit.

I stood over him, holding the bloody sword, expecting to feel an angry pride, a fierce satisfaction that one of my mother's murderers had died at my hands. And I did, but what I felt much stronger was a vicious nausea from the pit of my stomach that didn't so much fight its way up as explode out my mouth and all over Tiny's corpse. The sight of so much vomit and blood led to a second wave of my intestines revolting, but this time I managed to turn so my gut emptied onto the ground.

I thought my first kill would make me tough, but all it did was make me realize that I really didn't know the meaning of the word.

I stood and dry heaved, barely hearing the footsteps behind me. I spun, leading with my sword and was lucky enough to block Oaf's blade on its way to slice open my skull. It would have been even more impressive had I known the proper way to hold a sword, but I didn't, and the impact knocked the blade from my grip.

Now I stood weaponless against a soldier with a sword. The fact that I was just a kid hit me hard. An idiot kid who thought she could take on soldiers by herself. My righteous anger was replaced by fear. I couldn't beat Oaf this way. My only hope for survival lay in getting far away from him. I flapped my wings and took to the skies. Or I would have if I could have. Their camp was in a clearing, but the treetops surround it formed a canopy that nothing larger than a bird was flying through. I had to fly on a path parallel to the ground, maneuvering through the branches and the trunks.

Oaf, who turned out not to live up to his name, pulled out a bow and a quiver. I flew faster, ignoring the branches as they tore into my face and skin.

The graycoat raced after me, managing to shoot and run at the same time. I think the running threw off his aim, but not enough for my comfort. I felt the air ripple as an arrow passed close to my face.

I ignored everything that I could push and fly through. My face and arms were soon raked and bloody, but I couldn't risk stopping to do more than look back.

There was no sign of Oaf so I went faster, thinking I might get away, all the while blaming myself for being foolish enough to have gone after the graycoats with only a knife. And more so for not having slit their throats while they slept. Or at least taken their weapons before waking them.

I needed something to even things up. With a bow, I could pick Oaf off from the sky. Unfortunately, other than knowing a bow had a string, I had no idea how to make one. Or shoot it. I told myself that if I survived this, I'd learn.

Suddenly, I wondered if I had hit my head because around me the trees seemed to move by themselves. I stopped and stood on a high branch. Far behind and below me, Oaf trampled through the woods. He was far enough away that he looked like an insect. Hidden by the tree trunk, I looked in front of me where the leaves seemed to dance as if invisible hands shook them. A high-pitched whistling sound teased my ears. I walked along branches until I got close enough to see beyond the woods.

A river with impressively choppy rapids raced by, so wide that the trees on the other side appeared to be the size of toothpicks.

Ckuf. I swam like a rock. My ogre and pixie heritage combined to make my muscles denser than water. Simply put, I sink.

From stalking Oaf and Tiny, I knew that other pairs of graycoats patrolled both upstream and down. I had no way of figuring whether Oaf had a way of summoning them or worse, if he already had. In the woods, I'd never get far enough ahead of him. Yet moving along the river might be an invitation for more graycoats to shoot me out of the sky.

My only chance was to get across that river. Even a good swimmer would have a rough time of it in those choppy waters.

I climbed to the top of the nearest tree that wasn't shaking. Fear made sure I was shaking enough as it was. Wind makes flying dangerous for someone my size. A good updraft could carry me for miles, while a bad downdraft could send me crashing.

The winds seemed to blow along the same direction as the river. That was good. If I caught it just right I could angle my air path diagonally and make it across the water.

I leapt into the air as high as I could. My feet more than cleared the trees in front of me and I was airborne.

Pixie wings don't work like birds' wings. We don't glide well. It's more akin to a bee or hummingbird, requiring constant work to stay up, with smaller movements to change direction.

There were no problems getting to the river. The problem was staying over it. The wind made a tunnel of the air, which kept pushing me aside. I didn't have the strength to punch through it.

But maybe I could go over it.

I pushed and climbed, but the wind didn't let up. If anything, it got stronger. One big gust flipped me over and spun me around. I couldn't tell up from down, left from right.

I stopped moving my wings. It took a moment, but I started to plunge. Now I knew which way down was. With any luck, I'd manage to right myself before I hit the water.

Luck wasn't in a helpful mood. I hit the water and kept going down. I pushed and kicked to speed it up. It might seem odd, purposefully heading in the opposite direction of air, but it made sense. I can't swim, but I can walk. I wasn't too far from land.

I picked my best guess of which way the shore lay and let the current push me as I ran along the bottom, pulling against the water with my arms. I went with the same diagonal strategy I tried in the air, hoping to have better luck. My wings were hard and worked just as well in the water as the air.

My lungs burned, begging for air, but I couldn't stop. I wouldn't. I refused to die until all those who killed my mother were dead too.

White stars danced in front of me in the water, then everything turned dark. I felt something brush against me, then bump me, not once but three times. I guess the third time was the fix because my head broke the water's surface. No nectar has ever tasted as sweet as that first gasp of air.

I made it to the same side of the river that I'd left from, more crawling than walking, and moved as far away from the river as I could before my limbs gave out and dropped me on my stomach.

I lay gasping for air, but my breath was proving a more elusive quarry than I was. I heard hoof beats approaching. Quickly, I rolled over. What looked like an odd horse stared down at me. Odd because of the angular shape of its head, its overly large mouth, and its blue color.

"Not a good swimmer," it said, which was not particularly odd. Many animals in Faerie can talk if they make the effort to learn. "Seems a foolish thing to try, getting across my river."

"Your river?" I said.

"Oh, yes. Nothing can fly across it, although some call it Wind River. Few can swim across it except for little old Aughisky."

"You can swim that?"

"Oh yes. Didn't you see Aughisky out there helping you make it in?"

I didn't, but I felt his push. "I owe you my thanks, Aughisky."

"Yes, many owe Aughisky, but so few pay their debts. It's

why Aughisky left the family lake and went out on his own. Other Aughisky thought him mad, but Aughisky proved them wrong. Crossing lake easy. Crossing river hard. People willing to pay to cross. Now would the little, winged girl like to discuss what she owes Aughisky for saving her?"

"What do you want?" I asked, nervously. I had never seen a horse with sharp teeth smile before.

"So if Aughisky tells little wing thing what Aughisky wants, wing thing will give it to Aughisky?"

"I'll certainly consider it," I replied. "If I agree, then what I owe you for saving me is paid?"

"Aughisky supposes." The horse's mouth opened wide and revealing even more teeth than I'd first thought. All of them appeared long and sharp. Aughisky stepped toward me. I scurried back. It continued to move so I reached out to look for a weapon – a rock, a branch, something to defend myself with. My hand found something, and I pulled it up, only to feel it squish between my fingers.

I looked and realized I was holding something brown and mushy that likely was the insides of a person or animal at one time. I realized Aughisky had stopped his advance. I stood and the wind almost knocked me over again. I wasn't going to be flying any time soon.

"Liver is so repulsive. So unsavory. No good for no one, no good at all."

"How do you know it's a liver?" I asked.

"Aughisky knows."

"Do you know how it got here?" I asked, dropping it.

Aughisky had a hint of a smile on his long face that vanished so quickly I wasn't sure it was ever there. "How would Aughisky know that?"

I shook my hand, sending leftover pieces of innards flying. Aughisky jumped back like I had thrown a knife.

"Watch what you do. Aughisky did save your little life."

"And you want this liver gone?" I asked.

"Aughisky does."

I bent down and picked it up again. "Then we have a deal."

The horse's jaw dropped. "No. Wait. Aughisky didn't mean–"

But it was too late. I rushed down to the river and threw the liver in, but not before coating my hands in it, getting bits under my fingernails. The horse seems afraid of the liver, so it seemed wise. After all, our deal was for the liver, not any juices it might contain.

"Done," I said and started walking downstream, praying I wouldn't run into any graycoats before the wind let up or there was a way to cross.

I heard hoof beats and turned to watch Aughisky cantor up beside me.

"Little wing girl no want to cross river anymore?"

"Can't figure out how to do it safely here. I'll find another place that will work better," I said, walking faster. Aughisky kept up easily, an advantage of four legs over two.

"But Aughisky could take little wing girl."

"I'm not sure I could afford your price," I said.

Aughisky smiled again, this time wider. The sight of a horse with teeth as sharp as those of a dragon sent chills up my spine. "Aughisky always willing to negotiate. What do you have?"

"What do you want?" I countered.

"Perhaps little wing girl's name?"

"I'm a kid, not a toddler. I know better than to give you my name," I said.

"Aughisky told you his name. Be fair."

"I don't think Aughisky is your name. I think it is what you are," I said.

"Why little wing girl think that?"

"Because you referred to your family as the other Aughisky," I said.

The water horse laughed. "You smart. Aughisky foolish for

letting that slip. Doesn't mean we cannot come to agreement for passage over Wind River. Gold is always good."

"I've no gold," I said.

"Silver then."

"None."

"Any coin?"

I shook my head. "Sadly, no."

The horse looked at my throat. "What about necklace?"

It was pewter. Not worth much, but it had sentimental value. It was a gift from my pixie father on my last birthday. I thought about it, and I could hear old Thunderrod in my mind's ear telling me he could always buy me another so long as I survived.

"Deal. I'll give it to you once I'm safely on the other side," I said.

"No, too easy for you to run off, and then where will poor Aughisky be? Necklace first before passage."

I took it off and held it dangling by its chain. "Necklace for safe passage."

The water horse reached out with his mouth and plucked the necklace from my fingers with his lips. I had to force myself not to pull back. "Necklace for passage is what I said."

An arrow whizzed by my head, clipping my ear and Aughisky's mane. I turned to see Oaf lean out from behind a tree, notching another arrow. The wind probably just saved my life.

"Who be shooting at Aughisky?"

"One of Thandau's graycoats, and he's lining up his next shot. Time for running and swimming," I said.

"Aughisky thinks little wing girl is right. Get on!"

I did, and no sooner had I sat upon his back then we were off running down the shore. I barely got a hold of his mane before I looked back to see an arrow sticking out of the ground where we had stood.

Aughisky ran so fast and far that in moments, I could no longer see Oaf.

"Think Aughisky lost graycoat."

"Looks that way," I said.

"Foolish soldier, try to kill Aughisky. Not realize he on wrong side of food chain." Before I could say anything, he ran into the water. A rapid hit me hard enough to knock me over, but I didn't budge. I tried to move, but my lower limbs were caught fast.

"Aughisky, my legs –"

"Yes, Aughisky knows. Aughisky has special power, won't let rider get off."

I didn't like the way he said "get" instead of "fall", but before I could question this, he dove beneath the water. I barely had time to get a breath before we sank to the bottom of the river where Aughisky ran as easily as he had along the shore.

The horse could breathe underwater but I couldn't. I tried to get off, but Aughisky had told the truth about his sticking power.

Drowning is not a good way to die. I didn't survive the damn graycoats to get killed by a swimming horse.

I wrapped my right arm around Aughisky's neck and pulled. Even underwater I heard some pops from his spine adjusting. I tried to move my arm, but couldn't. The sticking magic extended to his neck.

Good. I dug my liver-coated hand into the skin there and felt it start to burn as I jammed my fingernails in. I took my free hand and rammed it into Aughisky's left eye. The horse screamed and tried to throw me off, turning the magic stickiness off. If I fell, I'd be stuck at the bottom of the river, so I held on with my legs and arms.

"Up," I glubbed with some of my little remaining air as I squeezed harder and wrapped my fingers around his eye.

The water must have carried my words well enough because

Aughisky swam to the surface.

"Your hands burn!" the water horse screamed. "Let go of Aughisky, you monster."

"Not until you take me to shore." I felt the water horse tense beneath me. "If we go under the water, your eye comes out. I may rip it out anyway just on principal."

"No, Aughisky needs his eyes. Aughisky make you a deal. You take hand from Aughisky's eye and Aughisky take you back to shore."

"No, I want to go to the far shore. And you will not get off that easily. You tried to kill me and broke our previous deal."

"Only because Aughisky hungry."

"You were going to eat me?" I said.

"Not all of you. Aughisky leave the liver. It is foul, poisonous thing."

"Well, you better come up with something better to offer me than passage only," I said, squeezing his eye.

"Aughisky doesn't know what you want. You tell Aughisky, and it shall be yours. Promise. Is better than deal. Never break promise. Break deals all the time."

"Whatever I ask? Your word?" I said.

"Yes, Aughisky's word is his promise."

A plan began to form in my mind and I smiled. I told Aughisky what I wanted.

The water horse nodded. "Aughisky can do that."

"You better or I will come back for you with a hundred livers," I said.

"No need to threaten. Aughisky's word is good."

The water horse swam to the far shore. I got both legs on dry land before I let go of his neck and eye.

Aughisky swam back into the river. Even if he broke his word, at least I made it across the river.

But the water horse kept his promise and went back to where we'd started. I kept pace with him on my side of the river. I made a little effort to pretend to be hiding but knew the graycoat would still see me. I didn't want him to give up the chase at this point because he thought I'd gotten away. Oaf was still there trying to figure a way across. Aughisky offered his services. They made a deal, and the graycoat climbed on. The water horse reared up, causing the graycoat to try to grab onto his flank where Aughisky's magic locked the soldier's hands in place, along with his legs. I guess he learned his lesson from me.

I squinted and strained to watch as Oaf was taken into the river. I couldn't hear Oaf over the winds, but I saw his face contort in a scream as he was dragged under. The screams were much shorter than those of my mother. I couldn't tell if tears accompanied them like my own when he and his ilk attacked me, but these silent screams were infinitely more satisfying.

Moments later, Aughisky surfaced back on my side of the river, a limp Oaf still stuck to his back.

I stepped forward to examine the soldier. He looked dead, but just to be sure I pulled his sword out of his scabbard and ran it through his black heart.

"See, Aughisky kept word."

"So you did," I said, taking Oaf's bow and quiver, as well as his sword belt and dagger. Oaf's weapons were the last part of the water horse's promise to me. Now I had a bow, and I would be able to kill the rest of my mother's murderers from a distance.

"May Aughisky eat now?"

"First return my necklace," I said.

"That was part of our deal for passage."

"For safe passage. You broke the deal. Return the necklace," I said.

"Pewter necklace worthless."

I held my hand out. "True, except for the fact that it is mine."

"Little wing girl fight Aughisky over worthless necklace?"

"Not if you give it to me," I said.

The water horse laughed. "Aughisky likes little wing girl." He retched and out came the necklace from his gullet onto the sand. "Have necklace with compliments. May Aughisky eat now?"

"Yes, Aughisky may eat now," I said.

The water horse reached back with his mouth and opened it wide. His sharp teeth tore Oaf's hand off. The water horse chewed and swallowed it in three gulps.

"Meat doesn't taste right dry." Aughisky carried Oaf's body into the rapids.

I sat and picked up my necklace, then watched as the waters turned crimson, then back to white. Aughisky did not surface again, but a lone liver did.

I headed in the same direction as the river. There were still more of Mama's killers to find and make pay.

Becoming Daemor

"The three of you have completed the training to become a Daemor. You are the best out of your fellow soldiers. Sadly, the only time we make a new Daemor is when we lose one of the old." Queen Mab bowed her head in a moment of respectful silence.

If there were three of us here, that meant three Daemor died. I felt awful for the elite soldiers of Mab's Army but I'd been training to join their ranks ever since I was recruited into Mab's rebel army.

Mab raised her head to look down from the dais at us. "Though we shall miss our departed sisters, we are prepared to welcome you three into our ranks."

That sounded too good to be true. Daemor were never just welcomed in. They had to perform some great feat after the training to prove themselves worthy of the rank.

Lillian the spriggan bowed. "My Queen, I will work hard to prove myself worthy of this honor."

"Though I have no doubt that you would, the offer is not being made." Lillian's face dropped. "Yet. Two of our sisters have been captured by graycoats and await execution on the morrow. The mission I offer the three of you is to get them back."

A booming yet beautiful voice rang from Smaze, the dragon next to me. "Where are they being held, my Queen?"

"In Carpathian."

"It sounds like a suicide mission," I said.

Queen Mab raised her eyebrows and stared at me. The Queen had a very imposing presence but I met her stare. "Why do you think that?"

"Carpathian is one of three of Thandu's stronghold cities, second in strength only to the capital itself. Its walls are thirty feet high and garrisons an entire legion of graycoats. Three against a legion is suicide."

"And you have a problem with suicide?"

"Yes, my Queen. I'm willing to risk death in a fight or to achieve a goal greater than myself, but to throw away any life needlessly – particularly mine – is foolish."

Mab stood and stared at me. When I didn't flinch beneath her glare, she nodded. "Good, because I agree with you. So we are going to give you all the intelligence we have on Carpathian and the three of you are going to put together then execute a rescue plan. Any questions?"

"Who are we bringing home?" Lillian said.

"The Daemor Kande and Elon. Are you all in?"

The Dragon, the spriggan, and I answered in unison, "Yes ma'am!"

Although I was glad my fellow soldiers were on board, I would've gone alone. After I had been fighting the graycoats on my own and trying to avenge what they did to Mama and me, I was captured and put into another slave camp. What happened there was not pretty. Kande saved my life and rescued me, then recruited me into Mab's army. I owed the woman from Earth my life. Elon was a horse that she brought over from Earth. Faerie's magic granted Elon intelligence. She had a fierce spirit and the heart of a horny trickster.

I would make sure the graycoats didn't kill Kande or her horse friend, no matter the cost. That wouldn't be suicide. It would be repaying a debt.

We poured over the intelligence, including estimates of troop strength, guard schedules, and a map of the town.

We disagreed on what our plan of action should be. Smaze wanted to launch a surprise attack by air, which might have worked had she been a pureblood fire dragon but she wasn't. Her father was a water dragon and her mother a fire dragon. She was able to combine the two magics and breathe out boiling water and steam. While that would hurt whoever it hit, it wouldn't spread the way fire would.

Lillian was convinced we could get a hold of a graycoat on guard duty and force him to bring us into the jail so we could rescue them. While that might get us in, it wouldn't do much for getting us out. And getting out was the whole point of a rescue attempt.

"You have a better idea, Razzorwing?" Lillian said, using my nickname.

"As a matter fact, I do."

One of the most important parts of Daemor training isn't how to fight. It's not even survival skills. It's memorizing a map of the Faerie paths. One of the Daemor, Tralla, has the mystical ability to make or control Faerie paths. She goes into great detail teaching us because it's not like a regular map as some of the paths are short but will take you across the world while others will slow down or speed up time for you when you come out the other end. You also have to be careful that you leave the same way you came or you could end up getting back to where you started centuries after you left. Or seconds.

Tralla had closed all the Faerie paths near the stronghold cities but closed is not the same is gone. She came with us to open the path but as a rule, Tralla is not allowed in battle. She was too valuable a resource and her death could single-handedly spell destruction for Mab's rebellion

My plan depended heavily on subterfuge, getting into the city unnoticed. While it might've been easier to leave Smaze waiting on the Faerie paths with Tralla, the dragon refused. This was her chance to become a Daemor and she wasn't letting anything stand in the way of that.

Smaze was a young and therefore relatively small dragon but she was still larger than a horse. Not exactly easy to hide. But not impossible either.

Plus, Smaze trained in going unnoticed like the rest of us and she was our key to getting into the city. I could fly over a thirty-foot wall, but my wings were not exactly silent and someone might hear and come looking. In a small town that wouldn't be much of a worry but in the city with the security of Carpathian, the soldiers would be alert for anything out of the ordinary.

We had arrived in the wee hours of the night. Smaze went first, breathing out steam that looked just like fog. There was already some on the open fields surrounding the city. Smaze just increased it, slowly and gradually over the course of an hour until it was thick. It moved in along one portion of the wall so it didn't appear to be a localized effect.

We waited for a pair of guards walking sentry duty to pass on the upper wall, climbed on Smaze's back and quicker than one would think possible, the dragon was up and over the wall. We landed in an alley in the working-class quarter of the city.

It was mostly people with families so we hoped there would be no one up and about so we could go undetected. It worked like a charm. At this part of the plan, it would have been nice to have Daemor badges. Not having them was the other reason we were chosen. Thandau had his mages put wards around each of his stronghold cities to detect the presence of a Daemor badge. If one came into the city, it would set off alarms and ruin any hope of surprise.

But the real reason I wanted a badge was because it had a special glamour charm built in. Daemor wear full body armor but the glamour makes it look as though they are dressed in skimpy tops and bottoms that show more skin than they protect. Mab believes it distracts the men who we typically fight and also makes them believe that we aren't protected. When they think they've delivered a terrible wound, the armor protects the Daemor and gives them a chance to strike a killing blow while the enemy has relaxed, thinking he's won.

This is the part of the plan that I found a tad distasteful. Lillian and I dressed up like ladies of the evening. It was a sad truth that in Thandau's Faerie, most women were reduced to the roles of virgin, mother, or whore. Men, particularly soldiers who hold the great physical power and weapons, tend to dismiss women as no threat. This was particularly true of the whore variety.

Neither of us were the smallest of women, at least in build. Lillian was three or four hands shorter than me, at least at the moment, but she had broad shoulders and thick muscles. I, of course, was even broader with larger muscles and rather well-endowed in the chest and seat department. While prostitutes did not have a uniform per se, there were a lot of commonalities in the outfits. One of the most popular was the one I wore. It was basically a long but not too wide ribbon of material that crossed my chest in an X formation, then wrapped around my nether regions.

It made me a little self-conscious although it shouldn't have. There are places in Faerie where people go without any clothes at all. It's just wearing the uniform of a woman who had sex for money bothered me. I couldn't imagine doing that. The only plus was I was able to wrap it so it didn't interfere with my wings at all.

"If I have to wear this, I don't see why you don't," I said.

"My outfit isn't any much better." It was basically a bra and panties. "Besides, if I wore that and had to fight, it would strangle me or dislocate my shoulders."

"I don't know what either of you are complaining about. You both look lovely for uprights." Which was the dragon's term for those of us with two arms, two legs, and one head. "You get to go out and do something. I have to hide here in the alley."

"Only until we get back," the spriggan pointed out.

The dragon rolled her eyes and blew out a puff of steam. She stood up in a corner of the alley and wrapped a cloak around her which instantly blended with the walls around her, making it look like she wasn't there.

Lillian and I left the alley.

"I guess we better go find us some graycoats," I said.

"Still doesn't seem right that we can't cut their throats," Lillian said.

"The blood would be too messy. Get all over us and make their uniforms useless."

"I suppose."

The next part of the plan was going to be difficult. To sneak further into the city, we were going to be searching for "clients" in the nonpeak hours. We needed to find at least two graycoats about our size. And they had to be off duty until after the execution or the plan wouldn't work.

Too many variables for my liking.

We went for several blocks with no potential soldiers as customers. As we passed a side street and a large, well-built goblin stepped out.

"Good evening, ladies. It's quite fortuitous us bumping into each other like this. I was just thinking of ways I could spend my latest windfall from a night of gambling and now here you are, an answer to my prayers."

The goblin wore trousers and a loose shirt and was well-built. He wasn't wearing a uniform but that didn't mean he wasn't a greatcoat.

"Hello there, handsome. You're looking for a good time, are you? Then we're your girls. You're a soldier, aren't you?" Lillian really got into her role, wrapping an arm around the goblin's waist.

The goblin, in turn, wrapped his arm around her shoulder.

"Bah. I'm better than a soldier. I'm an armorer. I make the swords for the soldiers."

Lily and I shared a look and I shook my head. An armorer wasn't going to work for the plan. Lillian disengaged and took a step back. "Oh, I'm so sorry. The Dark Lord himself subsidizes us, but only for his soldiers."

"So now he's putting restrictions on the oldest and most joyous of professions? Bah. No one need know. I won't tell." The goblin reached into his pouch and pulled out two gold coins. "I have far more money than a soldier. I'd be willing to give each of you one of these for an evening of pleasure."

Lillian made a big show, fawning over the coins and allowing me to get the goblin in a throat lock. I squeezed until he passed out. I dragged him back and laid the goblin in the alley, but not quite the way he had hoped for.

"Surely we can kill an armorer?"

I shook my head. "If they find his body, it raises alarms. We don't need anything giving us our presence away."

"Fine." Lillian bent down and took his purse off his belt. "But I'm sure we can put this to better use." Before I could say anything, Lillian added, "Besides if he woke up with a story about two whores who knocked him out while he was drunk and didn't rob him, that will raise suspicions as well."

True enough.

We walked further and stopped in a tavern. Drinkers there were sparse, maybe five people plus the barkeep. Fortunately, two of them were graycoats. A troll and a mixed breed that looked like he probably had some drawf and maybe some human in him. He had a beard. The troll was a gon, a graycoat sergeant. That would be helpful. We sauntered over to them and I sat to the side of the troll and Lillian to the side of the smaller one.

"You lads looking for a good time this evening?" I said.

The troll laughed. "If I were, I'd break you."

"I'd like to see you try," I purred. "The bigger the better for me."

"And you look plenty big to me," Lillian said to the bearded soldier who smiled at the compliment as men are want to do.

"That sounds very tempting ladies but after tonight, I'm broke until to the next payroll. Unless my big buddy over there is willing to loan me a few coins."

The troll laughed. "Sorry but I'm low on coin too. Unless of course, you two ladies would be willing to do a free service for the army."

Which no self-respecting prostitute would. "I'm sorry but we don't do freebies."

"Of course, there's another possible arrangement. Me and my big friend here have had a good evening. We've often talked and toyed with an idea that I think you two would be perfect for. We're somewhat tired of playing the whore. We were looking for two handsome men like yourselves to be our whores for the evening."

The troll leered. "So you're offering us a freebie?"

Lillian laughed and looked at me so I laughed, having no idea where she was going with this.

"Better than a freebie. We'll pay you."

She reached into the purse her stolen purse and pulled out two broken coins. "We will give you half a silver each."

The soldiers grinned and looked at each other like they just won a month's wages.

"Sure," the bearded one said.

"But as I said, you would be *our* whores. You would do what we tell you. We would tell you the positions we want, fast or slow, hard or gentle. You will do everything we tell you to."

The troll shrugged. "Certainly. We always have a lady's needs in mind. Now if you'll kindly give us our pay," he said holding out his large hand.

Lillian closed her hands upon the two half coins. "No, no,

no. I'm not going to pay my whore before he services me. You boys do a good job and maybe they'll be a couple coppers extra in it for you."

"Very good. Why don't you ladies get a room here and we'll head up to it."

"Sure, but the cost of the room is coming out of your pay," I said since we didn't want them anywhere near anyone else.

"I suppose we could always go back to the barracks," said the bearded one.

"Why? Do you have to go on shift?" Lillian said.

The bearded soldier put his arms around Lillian's shoulders leaned forward and kissed her neck. "Not until an hour before sundown tomorrow. We can play whore all day if you like."

"You think you can last all day?" Lillian said.

"I'm certain I'll last longer than you," he said.

"So claims every man."

"Then to the barracks it is."

"What, so your friends can all watch and pass us around like party favors? We're paying, so we get to switch places. That doesn't sound like switching places to me," I said. "We have a small room not far from here. We'll go there."

The troll stood up and he was a big one. I stood up next to him I couldn't even reach up to touch his ear.

"Then what are we waiting for? Let's go so we can be at these good ladies' service," the troll said.

The troll put his hand down on my back and I had to fight so my wings didn't twitch and cut him.

"I like your wings. I can't wait to see what they can do."

"Don't forget, tonight you work for me. Perhaps if you're good and make me happy, you'll find out."

Both men reached over for their tankards and drained them dry. We rubbed and stroked their arms and torsos as we walked through the streets to keep them distracted so they didn't think about it too hard about what was happening

"This is a nice neighborhood. You actually work out of here with all the families?" the troll said.

"We're very discrete. The door to our room is in an alley and it's off my sister's apartment. What we pay her covers half of her husband's rent for the whole thing so they're happy to have us

"Aren't you worried we might wake them or their children? I like to be loud," asked the troll.

"Me too," said the bearded soldier.

"Me three," purred Lillian.

"Fortunately, the walls are especially thick," I said. "This is us up here." We turned into the alley.

"That's odd. There's a fog just here," said the bearded one.

"It's spooky. Would you two gentlemen mind going first and making sure is nobody waiting in the alley for us? Occasionally we have customers come by wanting freebies," Lillian said.

"Not to worry, my dears. No one is going to ruin this evening for us," the said troll as he and the bearded one marched to the end of the alley where suddenly Smaze opened her eyes.

The two soldiers startled and turned to run. We had switched partners. It really wasn't mean of me. The small bearded one came at me. I punched him in the jaw and he went out like a candle.

"So you think you'll waylay us? Smooth but foolish move, especially for the little one to come after me," said the troll.

"Who are you calling little?" Lillian said and suddenly grew so large that she towered over the troll. The shock of seeing the spriggan take her larger form made the troll freeze long enough for her to knock him out as well. Which is why it wasn't mean of me to take the bearded one.

Spraggins can't stay in their large form all the time but they can stay long enough to do some serious damage.

"Reminds me of working for grandpa." Lillian's family ran all the crime in her town before Thandau's army ransacked the place and killed off a lot of her family and sent them to the camps where they were separated. She doesn't know if she's the only one still alive or if her parents or siblings survived.

We dragged the unconscious soldiers to the back of the alley and stripped them out of their uniforms. Unfortunately, the bearded one, while about my height, was not quite as broad as me. I was barely able to squeeze into his uniform. Lillian at her full spriggan size was having a similar issue with the troll's uniform. Fortunately, she was only a few inches taller and he was broader so his pants only came to midcalf.

Both soldiers' boots didn't fit us which is why we had brought our own. This allowed Lillian to tuck her pants in so no one would notice they were too short. We would have brought entire uniforms except for the fact that city graycoats uniforms were charmed and they had to be renewed on a weekly basis. If we walked into a barracks with outdated charms, it would set off alarms.

Smaze had the gift of producing vapors that could do more than just scald or cause fog. One of them could knock people unconscious. Enough would keep them that way for a day. Smaze made sure they had enough.

"I'll see you two at the jail," Smaze said lifting up a rainwater drain and somehow managing to squeeze herself through a very small space. She'd make her way through the sewage tunnels.

"With luck, her stink won't give her away," Lillian said.

"Let's hope."

We put on the uniforms and applied makeup and prosthetics. We made Lillian look like a very large troll and I put on a Brown wig and a false beard to match the owner of my uniform. We wouldn't fool anyone they knew, but for our plan to work, the soldiers wouldn't know whom we were supposed to be impersonating anyway.

Graycoats didn't hide, especially in a stronghold city. We hid the soldiers as best we could beneath some trash and marched out of the alley and onto the street. Completing our disguises had taken quite a while and it was past eight bells. The execution was scheduled for nine. We marched ourselves all the way to the jail and waited nearby and out of sight in a doorway, standing at attention so people would think we were on guard duty if they noticed us

At half bells, graycoats marched Kande and Elon out. Instead of her typical blue jeans and chainmail bra glamour, Kande was dressed in a shapeless sack with her wrists and ankles shackled together with a chain linking the two. It was tight enough that she had to bend over to walk. Elon the horse had a similar set up except her connecting chain was shorter, ensuring that she couldn't kick at anyone behind her.

It was now or never. We stepped out from the doorway and marched towards the six soldiers.

Lillian had a deeper voice so she did the talking.

"They sent us for backup because of how tricky these Daemor can be. We were told to make sure you bring their badges and weapons. They want to make a show of it."

A couple soldiers chuckled.

"Figures that they won't trust us to do a basic job. I can understand wanting to make a show of killing these stitches. The whoring Daemor have been giving us trouble for far too long. You two, go get the weapons."

Two of the graycoats walked back into the jail where a mist poured in through the back window, courtesy of Smaze. The pair of enemy soldiers passed out and hit the floor hard.

"What the inferno?" the leader said.

While he was staring at the fallen men, I hit him on the back of the head and he toppled unconscious.

The remaining three graycoats were all significantly smaller than Lillian in her large form. They were even shorter than me and we had our swords out, not to mention pointed their way.

"Don't even think about it," I said, stepping forward to disarm their blades and any other weapons they had. Kande looked up at me and smiled.

"Razorwing, glad to see you."

"You too, Kande."

We herded the soldiers so they were between the wall of the jail and Lillian. I took the keys off the graycoat I knocked out and undid our comrades' shackles.

"Give us our badges and we'll get out of here." Kande was bruised and bloody all over and barely able to walk.

Elon nodded her head and whinnied in an agreement then walked over to stomp on the unconscious leader a few times.

"It's not that simple. The detection wards around the city will go off when the badges leave, same as if they came in. So the plan is for the two of you to go with Smaze and get out of here. Tralla is waiting to open up the path as soon as you get close," I said.

Kande squinted at me. "And what about the two of you? How are you getting out?"

"That's yet to be determined. But in order to give you enough time to escape, we're going to head toward the execution in your place."

Elon looked at me and Lillian then whinnied at Kande. The human seemed to understand the horse. Personally, I thought it was rude. Despite also coming from Earth, Elon had been here long enough for the natural magic of Faerie to raise her intelligence and mutate her form enough that she could talk if she wanted to. She just didn't care enough to try. "How's that going to work? Neither of you looks anything like us."

I took out the glamour additions. "We hook up these to your badges and whoever is wearing them will look exactly like the two of you."

"So you are *literally* going to take our place."

Lillian chuckled. "Not us. These three."

"We are not leaving you." Elon shook her mane like she was okay with it. "With my healing factor, I'll be in fighting shape in no time."

Then Kande stumbled.

"You will, but not in time to be of any use in a fight now."

She grumbled but realized I was right.

I went into the jail holding my breath and came out with their badges, Kande's sword and a gun she brought with her from Earth. It's called a .357 Magnum and can put quite a big hole in somebody. She went back to Earth at one point and brought a ridiculous amount of ammunition back with her and then had a spell cast that automatically reloaded her gun from the ammo storage. I went back out and handed Kande her sword and gun. She took the blade.

"You keep the gun. I've shown you how to use it. You guys may need it. Give it back to me when you catch up with us."

I nodded at her.

Lillian had shackled the three men the same way Kande and Elon had been and then put additional shackles so one of the men was locked to the waist of the other one. We stuck the badge on the rear solder and the two of them looked like Elon. The Daemor badges were keyed to the blood, or what Kande called DNA, of the Daemor so they were useless to anyone else. The only function the soldiers or I could access was the glamour.

I put the other badge on the remaining soldier's back and he looked just like Kande. Lillian and I took deep breaths and bound, gagged then dragged the three unconscious soldiers into a cell.

Neither of the rescued Daemor wanted to leave us but we managed to convince them they had to. They've been beaten and abused pretty bad by their captors. Neither one was in any shape for a prolonged battle. They were having trouble just walking. And the only reason they could still do that I'd bet was because they wanted them to be able to limp to their own execution.

We made sure the disguised soldiers knew that if they tried to run or give away our plan, that we'd slit their throats.

The guy who was the front half of Elon kept trying to lead us down wrong streets, but we had memorized the map of the city too well for that to work.

As we got nearer, the execution site crowds we encountered crowds. They saw us with what they thought were Daemor prisoners and several people cheered. Some of them did it in bloodthirst and others did it because they felt they had to.

We were still a good way from the chopping blocks when Lillian whispered to me, "You think that's enough time for them to get out?"

"It better be. I say we grab the badges and bail as soon as we have to push through that mob up ahead and hope in the confusion we make it over the wall without becoming pincushions."

Before we could grab and run, the crowd suddenly turned away from jeering at us toward the raised chopping block platform and a chant rang out from the crowd. Lily and I exchanged looks of confusion which then turned into ones of terror when we heard what the crowd was chanting.

"Thandau!"

"Chuf." I wanted to throw up. "Holy frag."

Although it wasn't the capital city, I guess the execution of two Daemor was enough to bring the Dark Lord here to us.

Lillian started to bolt but I grabbed her huge wrist and held her in place. Not that I didn't want to run too, but Thandau by himself had taken on entire battalions and won, slaughtering hundreds in his wake.

"We have to get out of here now."

"As soon as we pull the badges, he'll slaughter us just for

fun."

"So leave the badges. The speeches and taunting should last at least an hour. That's enough time for us to get gone."

"But our mission was to rescue the Daemor and make sure their badges didn't fall in graycoat hands.

"We completed half the mission. There is no purpose served by us dying too."

Lillian was right but she was also wrong. Ahead of us was the very embodiment of evil, the conqueror of Faerie. The great destroyer. The man responsible for creating the army whose soldiers killed my mama. No one has ever been able to stop him. The only ones who stood up to him were Mab, her rebel army, and the Daemor. One of the Daemor's greatest weapons was their badges. If Thandau figured out a way to create them for his side, or worse, negate them for ours, the rebellion was over. Nothing would stand in Thandau's way.

Still, there was no reason for *both* of us to die.

"Stay with me until we do the handoff of the prisoners. Then you get out of here."

"What are you going to do?" Lillian said.

I wanted to kill Thandau but knew enough to realize that was beyond my ability.

"I'll stay long enough for you to get away. Then I'll take the badges and make a break for. With any luck, I'll get away. If I'd don't, keep an eye out from the path and I'll at least get the badges outside of the city. You guys make sure the badges go with you."

"And you'll catch up to us?"

"Of course," I lied. I wasn't getting away. After what happened to me and mama, I turned on a path for vengeance. Joining Mab's army helped me focus past that. Sure, the driving force in my life was to rid Faerie of Thandau and his army but I had other thoughts too. I didn't wake up every day seething with hate and anger anymore. I was taught honor. And sacrifice.

Now we'd see just how well I learned that last lesson.

I wasn't going to just lay down and die either. If I could somehow sneak away, I might have a chance. If our intel was correct, most of the army was here at the execution. That left a skeleton crew guarding the walls and the gates.

As we got closer, I saw Thandau sitting on a golden throne. He was smaller than I imagined, maybe twice my height with gray skin and horns that didn't look demonic but weren't quite like any other animal I've ever seen. Even this far from the tyrant, I could feel power coming off him in waves. Once again, I debated I contemplated a direct confrontation but even with Kande's weapon, one of the few guns that works long term in Faerie, I didn't have a chance. Thandau would swat me down like an insect beneath a boot.

As Lillian pointed out, we'd completed half the mission. It was up to me to take care the other half and going out in the blaze of glory or whimpering wasn't going to get it done.

Which is when an idea came to me and I turned and whispered to Lillian. "I have a plan."

"You going to make me fight the tyrant by your side, aren't you?" Lillian said.

"Nope, but here's what I want you to do." I outlined my plan.

Lillian nodded and started walking slower so she could disappear from our procession.

I handed off the chains to the Executioner's procession. The path to the chopping block was through a darkened corridor which had a door. I waited until they dragged our glamour disguised dupes into the darkness and pulled the badges off of each of them, backed away slowly then made my way through the crowd.

In the darkness, it sounded like the Executioner's procession took their turns beating those who were about to die just for the sadistic fun of it.

I'd managed my way to the outside of the crowd. Another few seconds and I would have gotten away clean, but one of the Executioner's procession ran out of the tunnel onto the chopping block podium.

"They're gone!"

Thandau rose up his golden throne and wrapped his hand around the torso of the processionary and lifted him up.

"Where did the Daemor go?"

"They walked into the tunnel but there are only three of our soldiers there now."

Thandau smashed the processionary down on the platform next to the chopping block.

"The processionaries will replace the scheduled victims."

The fallen processionary groveled. "No, my Lord. I have been loyal. I will find them and get them back for you."

"One failure is all you are allowed."

The tyrant pulled a huge broadsword out of his scabbard – it was as long as I was tall – and brought it down, separating the processionary's head from his shoulders.

Thandau turned to the executioner. "Keep the masses entertained while I find the Daemor."

Thandau leapt down from the stage into the middle of the crowd who quickly ran so the ground was empty when he landed.

If my plan was going to work, it was now or never. I placed Alon's badge on the back of my ribbon belt and Kande's on the back of my collar and activated the glamour spells. It wasn't perfect but it looked as if Kande was riding on the horse's back. I had vanished from sight so I stripped off my graycoat shirt, held onto it, and ran. On foot, I'm almost as fast as a horse at least in the short distance and by using my wings to help I was even faster.

I bowled over a graycoat as I headed toward the wall, to make sure I would be noticed.

I was.

The soldier shouted and Thandau's attention was on me. I leapt and landed sideways on a wall, pushed off and landed on a roof on the other side of an alley. I could see the illusion and it looked as though the horse was running with only her rear legs, which is why we'd used two soldiers to impersonate Elon. I angled myself so my rear faced them and hoped in the heat of the chase, it would go unnoticed.

I dare to look back. Thandau was running after me, his troops trailing behind him.

The Dark Lord was much faster than a horse, so I got to the edge of the roof and leapt as high as I could and flew off into the air.

"The damned horse can fly?!" Thandau lifted up his sword and pointed it at my glamours. A mystic bolt shot from the bladed and I banked a hard left. I only survived because he was aiming for Elon's head and the bolt missed me by the length of my forearm.

Arrows were filling the air around me so I climbed higher. Below me, Lillian was almost to the Faerie path, running as fast as her big legs could carry her. She too was faster than a horse. When she got to where the path was, Tralla opened it and the spriggan disappeared

I flew towards the wall and dove down outside. Once below the wall, I pulled the Daemor badges off of me and threw them ahead. The glamours turned off and they set off the alarm that indicated that they left the city. I landed on the wall, quickly putting the uniform top back on.

Lillian had relayed my plan. Now that the illusions of Kande and Elon vanished, the real ones came out of the Faerie path and stood so they could be seen. Thandau was almost to the wall. Since I looked like a graycoat, I pointed and shouted in my deepest voice, "Emperor, they have made it out of the city!"

In a much deeper voice than I could ever manage, Thandau's

voice boomed, "Well, get after them you fool!"

Which is exactly what I was hoping would happen. I leapt over the wall without using my wings. I landed disturbing my weight is best I could. I didn't injure myself but it was a hard landing. I sprinted towards the path, bending briefly to pick up the badges as I passed them.

A turn of my head revealed the soldiers scaling down the wall on ropes to join me in the chase. Fortunately, the archers thought I was a graycoat and didn't fire my way.

As I got closer, all five of my comrades were standing outside the path, ready to kill or do battle. I didn't want them attacking me by mistake, so I tore off my headgear and wig. They saw my pink hair and Smaze flew towards me, picked me up in her talons and airlifted me onto the path. Tralla, Lillian, Kande, and Elon followed. Tralla looked back to see Thandau had overtaken all his troops and was a hundred or so horse lengths from us. Tralla smiled and waved then closed the path as Thandau was leaping through the air at us, screaming in anger and frustration. The path shut and cut him off. Another few seconds and he would've had us.

I will tell you there was much celebrating that night. The next morning, the five of us were hung over when we were called into Mab's throne room. I won't bore you with the details of the ceremony but when it was over I had a Daemor badge of my own, as did Lillian and Smaze.

I had finally become one of my heroes.

Beneath Darkness

When darkness fell, I tripped over it and stubbed my toe. At least no one could see me embarrass myself. It could have been worse and no doubt would be before long.

Magiks that black out an entire battlefield are rarely ever good things.

The air had taken on an inky quality. It wasn't so much smoke as solid shadow. It seemed safe to breathe as I hadn't dropped dead yet.

I needed to find cover fast and flying was out. My wings may be sharp as swords and able to cut through tree limbs, but my head would be smashed open like a melon if it hit a trunk. I had enough trouble with my brains on the inside. I didn't want to see, even if there was enough light, what would happen with them on the outside. Of course, I might just crash into a hill. My chest is ample enough to cushion me, but it would still hurt, especially with an armored bra.

I crawled on hands and knees instead, finding my way by touch and smell. If I smelled death and corpses on the breeze, I went the other way.

My movement was probably louder than it should have been, but as near as I could tell before the lights went out, the nearest of Thandau's forces was five stones' throws away. That could be changing quickly however.

Luckily, I found a trench. Old fashioned warfare, but still effective.

"Hello to the hole," I whispered. If there was no answer, I'd have to debate about going in. One, I didn't want to be ambushed. Two, it might mean it was filled with dead soldiers. If I find a man's body when I'm feeling around in the dark, I want it to be warm and willing, not cold and bloody.

"Hello, yourself," came a voice. "What's the password?"

Damn. I was late to the briefing this morning. Was it just this morning when this all started? I racked my memory for the phase. "For the fate of Faerie."

"C'mon in," said the voice. "All the comforts of home, except without the comfort part. How is it out there?"

"Dark," I replied, climbing down.

The voice snorted. "Thank goodness we have such good intel. I can rest easy now."

"Then my work here is done," I said.

"I'm Neval. Who are you?" he said.

"They call me Razorwing," I said. My real name is Terrorbelle, but when I got into the Daemor, Kande, a woman from Earth, saddled me with that nickname. And it fits. And it's safer to use a taken name.

"Well, Razorwing, any idea which side let loose this black mess? Cause I sure as Hells don't remember this from the morning briefing.""At least you were paying attention," I joked. "Honestly, could be us or them. I just hope it's affecting them just as much as it is us. Cause if they can see through this ebony muck, we are in some serious trouble. I can't even make out the nose on my face, let alone you."

"You ain't missing much. At least that's what my wife tells me," Neval said with a soft chuckle. "You, on the other hand, sound gorgeous enough to make a man sit up and beg."

"Ha. I've always felt I look better in the dark, but that doesn't mean I can't make a man beg. Usually for mercy when my sword is at his throat," I said.

"Remind me never to get you mad."

"Sorry, you're on your own there. Too busy with the war and all," I said.

Our conversation ran cold as the sound of screams assaulted our ears. We both recognized the sounds of a soldier's death knell. It didn't end quickly.

"What in the Hells was that?" Neval whispered.

"Don't know, but whatever it is it has big jaws and claws," I said quietly.

"How...?"

"I have exceptional hearing," I said. Once you hear the sound of flesh ripped by teeth and talons you don't easily forget it. The sounds changed and my blood froze in my veins. "It's coming this way."

What echoed like exceptionally sized feet, numbering at least four, were padding their way across the battlefield.

"What should..." started Neval, but I lunged forward and felt around his face until I was able to cover his mouth to shut him up. Whatever this thing was, it was able to navigate in total darkness. It might be able to see, or smell, or sense heat, or maybe even had some sort of sonar. But maybe it used sound and I didn't want us to become its next targets.

Neval caught on and I was able to let go. Unfortunately, he started to pull his sword from its scabbard and it made a scraping noise.

The padding of the paws stopped.

"Ckuf," I swore. "What kind of weapons and fortifications do you have in here?"

"I thought we were supposed to be quiet?" he rasped.

"Doesn't matter. It heard you and it's coming in stealth mode," I said.

"Fecalation," he said. "Got a couple of spears, a shovel, my sword and a dagger. My crossbow is out of ammo, but it'd make a nice club. Other than that, it's a big hole. Hadn't had time to do anything else."

"Hand me a spear," I said, placing my hand on his shoulder. I felt the shaft bump against my forearm and grabbed it. "You take that half of the hole..." I touched the shoulder furthest from me and placed my back against his side. He spun so his back touched mine. "I'll take this one."

"Today's as good a day as any to die," said Neval, trying to bolster up his courage.

"Not as good as tomorrow. Or the day after," I said. "This thing is on foot, not flying. It'll probably jump and come down on us from above."

"Got it," he said and I could feel him bring his spear upright and move it side to side slowly.

I was glad he didn't ask me how I knew because I was guessing. For all I knew this thing might burrow through the ground and come up underneath us.

We waited in silence for minutes that passed slower than hours. I think Neval was close to cracking when he spoke.

"I think I know what this might be," whispered Neval. "A gloomer."

"Which is?" I asked. Silence was a better option, but the last thing I needed was the guy at my back having a breakdown. Besides, maybe the info might help us.

"Monster that creates a darkness to hunt in. I heard stories when I was a kid," said Neval.

"Did the stories mention how to kill it?" I asked hopefully. There still wasn't any sign of any creature, gloomer or otherwise.

"Nope. Apparently few people who meet one survive to tell the tale."

"You're a lot of help," I said.

"Hey, at least I brought the spears and dug the hole. You don't like it, give me my spear and go somewhere else," Neval said.

"Love to but..."

The creature attacked by dropping from above like I predicted and it came on Neval's side. I heard it a spilt-second before it landed and shouted a warning that wasn't soon enough.

I heard the sound of something impaling flesh, then felt Neval being lifted up behind me.

I spun, ducking low and lunged with the spear in hopes of not further impaling Neval. I missed the creature's torso, but swung the spear outward and hit something that felt like a leg. I quickly pulled back and jabbed forward. I felt the tip bite deep into flesh and was rewarded with another scream, but there was no way that screech came from a person. I heard Neval hit the dirt as the thing dropped him.

I tried to pull the spear out for a second stab, but the monster moved and the spear snapped. I got the larger piece, but not my wish. The thing was still alive.

"Sound off," shouted Neval.

"Yo," I said.

Next, the monster bellowed in pain as Neval balanced the battle scales by impaling the creature with his spear. I heard big feet shuffling and wood snapping.

"My spear broke," said Neval.

"Mine too. Time for blades," I said pulling out my long and short swords. I also flexed my wings. "This thing can see us or the next best thing, so keeping quiet helps it more than us. Keep talking so we don't kill each other."

"How about an inspiring battle song," Neval joked.

"Yeah, maybe we can sing it to death," I said.

I heard the wooden fragment from my spear hit dirt behind me. I didn't have time to turn, but I'm more deadly from behind. By reflex, my wings extended up and out. I felt my right one slice through flesh until it was stopped by bone. My wings can move with a speed that rivals a hummingbird, so I flexed and wing sliced again, putting more muscle behind it. My wing rethreaded the same wound, once, twice, a dozen times before the creature could react, slicing away in the blink of an eye, until my wing came through the other side. Its front paw, hand, or whatever fell and blood spurted like water through a tube.

If the sound it made was any indication, it wasn't happy. In its anger, the creature moved forward instead of retreating. I started beating my wings as fast as I could and it walked right into them. Kande had often remarked that when I used my wings as weapons it looked like I had a pair of buzz saws on my back. I ended up gutting the creature and it fell over, hopefully drawing its last breath.

"Move away. I'm coming toward you," I said.

"What in the Hells was that noise?" asked Neval.

"That was me. The creature is dying, but could still hurt us. I suggest we get on the top of this hole and stay out of its way until the Reaper claims it," I said.

"I'm kind of holding my innards in hopes of stopping them from becoming my outers. I'm not going to be able to climb and do that at the same time," said Neval.

"I'll lift you out," I said.

"A little thing like you?" said Neval.

I laughed. "I haven't been called little by anyone smaller than an orge since I was five."

"How old are you now?" asked Neval.

"Fifteen," I said. By most Faerie customs, I was an adult including my ogre and pixie heritages.

"I have a daughter your age. I guess you're old enough to know what you can and can't do," said Neval.

"Depending on the day," I said, picking him up with one arm under his shoulders, the other beneath his knees.

"I used to carry my wife like this when we were younger," he said.

"I won't tell her if you don't," I said. The creature started to thrash and I felt Neval stiffen. I still didn't want to fly blind and I couldn't climb carrying Neval. Fortunately, there was a compromise. I ran while beating my wings and I was able to literally run up the walls.

"Wow," he said when we were at the top.

I smiled, not that he could see me. "Let me check your wound."

"Gloomer got me good," he said.

I ripped his shirt open and felt around. He was cut deep, but despite Neval's opinion of what his hands were doing, nothing was hanging out. "I'm not a healer, but it seems serious enough. If we get you to the medics, you should be fine." I pulled a battle patch out of my waist pack, pinched the wound tight, and put it on. The battle patch adhered itself, started the tissue healing and kicked out some serious painkillers.

"That's amazing. I feel better already. Where'd you get it?" Neval asked.

"Standard issue battle patch," I said.

"Not for my unit. What are you, a general?" he asked.

"Naw, I work for a living. I'm in the top squad," I said trying not to brag. It really wasn't fair. Even if Neval was the best warrior in his unit, he'd never make the Daemor. He couldn't pass the physical without a gender changing spell.

"I can see why after what you did to the gloomer. I guess I shouldn't complain about not getting a battle patch since I got to use one anyway," said Neval.

"That'd be my take," I said, but he got me wondering. I know the battle patches cost Mab a fortune, but I thought she had issued at least one to everyone in her army. I'd mention to her next chance I had.

The sounds below had finally stopped.

"You think the gloomer's dead?" asked Neval.

"I'm willing to wait a few more minutes. But we don't know for sure it's a gloomer," I said.

"Yeah, we do. Look at the sky," he said. Above the faintest wisps of midday sun were starting to cut through the darkness. "We killed it and light returns. It's a gloomer."

"What's this *we* stuff?" I teased.

"I'm the one who distracted it for you. And they were my

spears," he said.

I grinned. "Fair enough. Any way to speed this along, so we can see again?"

"The tail of the gloomer is what spills out the shadows, at least according to the tales my grandmother told me. Supposedly you can cut off the tail and tie it off at both ends, then untie one to make things dark," he said.

"I thought you said you had never heard of anyone who had killed one," I said.

"I said the same thing to my grandmother. She pointed out that they die of natural causes same as anything else. She even claimed her grandmother had a tail."

"It might make a nice trophy at that. I'm going to go get it," I said.

"Be careful, Razorwing," he said.

"I will, Neval," I replied and jumped back in. I was starting to be able to see partial images of the world around me. I was able to make out the gloomer. It was vaguely reptilian, almost totally black but with the body shape of a bear. It looked dead, but I had seen too many friends killed by someone they thought was dead. I moved around behind its still form and hacked its head off with my longsword. It only took me two swings.

Next, I turned my attention to the tail. It was about the length of my arm, but only as thick as a serpent. I knotted off both ends with leather ties and sliced where it attached to the body. A little shadow leaked out, but overall Neval's grandmother seemed right on the money.

The darkness had receded to the point where I could see as well as during a foggy dusk. I floated up and out of the hole to hover in front of Neval. I was interested to see what he looked like. Hopefully, our medics weren't far. Pixie wings, even when they are as big as mine, were not designed to carry someone my size very far, so my flying is strictly a short distance deal. Especially ferrying someone.

Neval was smiling until I got closer. Then he scampered backwards and pulled his sword.

"What's the matter? I'm not that scary," I said.

"You're a Daemor!" Neval was pointing at the metal emblem under the midpoint where the glamour of my armored bra cups joined. The Daemor symbol was a black raven on a silver circle.

"I told you that," I said.

"No, you said you were in the top squad. I figured you for a Destroyer," said Neval.

"But the Destroyers are the enemy and…" I stopped short when I noticed his gray uniform. Neval was in Thandau's army. I chuckled bitterly. What were the odds of both sides choosing the same password on the same day? Since it was what both sides claimed they were fighting for, I guess not that high at all.

"You'll never take me alive," he said.

"I worked too hard to patch you up to kill you now," I said, landing well out of reach of his blade.

"I thought Daemor slaughtered on sight. The Destroyers do," said Neval.

"Propaganda mostly," I said. War is hell and soldiers do things they are ashamed of later in order to survive. "We're fighting for different reasons."

"I'm fighting to save my family," said Neval. "If I mess up, Thandau will have them slaughtered in punishment."

"That's horrible," I said.

Neval looked at me with a confused expression. "Mab doesn't hurt your family for your mistakes?"

"No. We're fighting to save them from being killed by your army," I said.

"I'm not doing this willingly. I was conscripted when they conquered my town," he said.

"Defect. Come over to our side," I said.

"Can't, not if the price is my family," said Neval.

I wanted to say we'd get his family, rescue them, but I

couldn't lie to him. We were barely holding our own using guerrilla tactics. There was no way we were going to be able to liberate a town behind enemy territory, so I just nodded. "We still need to get you medical attention."

"I won't be taken prisoner. If I don't return and they don't find a corpse, it's a death sentence for my wife and daughters." Made sense and made sure the troops didn't run off or go AWOL as Kande was fond of saying. "It's better if you kill me."

"If that's how you feel about it," I said, pulling out a dagger and throwing it at him. I saw his eyes go wide with fear the second before the hilt smashed his jaw and put out his lights.

There is a bond between those who fight side by side that someone who's hasn't been in a battle will never understand. I wasn't going to let Neval die and I couldn't let his family be killed either.

I came up with a plan. It was dangerous, foolhardy, and downright stupid. Mab would never approve, so I had no intention of ever telling her.

Once natural darkness fell, I dragged, carried, and flew the unconscious Neval behind enemy lines. I managed to get him to within sight of a graycoat camp. I laid him down and fixed a long fuse to a torch. I lit it and ran like Thandau himself was chasing me. Five minutes later, the torch flared to life and I was far enough away that they would hopefully never catch me.

I smiled as I pictured Neval's face when he woke up. I said a silent prayer that he and his family would survive the war and that we would not meet again until it was over. Because if we did, I might have to kill him and I already have enough deaths on my conscience.

Heart's Desire

"Walk away, forget you ever saw me, and I'll grant you your heart's desire," said the man in the graycoat officer's uniform. The gold trim marked him as being more dangerous than two dozen soldiers. It meant he was a mage. Worse, I had no idea what kind of magic he wielded.

"You could restore my mother to the way she was before." I hesitated to say back to life because poor Mama had already been through a false rebirth as one of the undead and she didn't deserve it again.

The mage knew exactly what I meant. "I'm afraid restoring the dead to life is beyond my abilities."

"And how about freeing Faerie of Thandau and his tyranny?"

"If I could do that, do you think I would be serving him in the Army? I'm not talking about granting a wish. I'm not a jinn. I'm talking about granting your heart's desire made real in the flesh."

"So you grant me a little gift and I'm supposed to shirk my duty and betray the Daemor? I don't think so. I suggest you surrender and put on the manacles." I reached into my pack and pulled out a pulled out some chains that would inhibit his magical abilities.

"I've heard how Mab and you Daemor treat graycoats. I'd be better off committing suicide."

"Well if you insist, but would you be quick about it?"

The officer mage chuckled, then closed his eyes yet somehow seemed to be staring at me.

When he reopened his lids he relaxed. "Impressive baubles those Daemor badges. Interferes with magic attacks on you, although not total protection. How about you come over here and put the manacles on me yourself."

My sword was long and sharp and as I stepped forward, I kept the tip pointed at the officer mage until it touched his throat.

"Try anything and you'll end up missing out on your chance at a fair trial."

I reached forward to place the manacles on the mage when his hand snapped around and grabbed hold of my fingers. I felt a jolt of magic jump from him to me.

Before I could run the graycoat through, he fell to his knees and put his hands behind his head.

"I saw your heart's desire and I think we can do business, which is why I've already granted it to you. However, it will vanish should I die. And I can also take it away from you at any time so I would keep that in mind before doing anything that would harm me."

"What are you babbling about?" Nothing had happened. "Your little spell didn't do anything."

The mage grinned and made a motion with his left hand in the air and suddenly a mirror larger than me was floating there.

"I beg to differ Daemor. Look."

I did.

It had to be some trick but when I looked down at my body it had changed. I've always been a mix of my two heritages, leaning a little more toward the ogre than the pixie. But now I wasn't broad and big. I was slender and….

"You made me beautiful."

"I would argue that you were beautiful before but sometimes people cannot see that about themselves so they desire to be something they're not. Something they feel they were denied. However, you are quite willowy and lovely. And you can stay that way. All you have to do is forget you saw me and let me go. Think about it. My power is to grant people's heart's desires. What possible harm could I be to the Daemor?"

I stared at my reflection. I hated it but he was right. This is what I had always wanted to look like from the time I was a little girl – thin and good-looking. The mage had a point. His power was fairly benign. Would it really be so bad to let him go? Especially when I had already taken care of the only other graycoats I found in the area.

Just as I was about to ask for his word that he would not use his powers to harm me or anyone else, there was a rustling in the woods that turned into booming as small trees were knocked aside as if they were sunflowers. A huge beast of a man who was as wide across as I was tall swiped a battleaxe and lopped off most of a large tree. He had purple skin and tattoos on his face and arms. I'd never seen anyone like him before – he looked like a mix of ogre and orc without really being like either of them. Maybe a drop of giant blood to give him that size. He wore a graycoat uniform and held a chain which he pulled and fifty slaves followed. They were all different races, their legs chained to assure they could barely take a step. Forget about running to escape.

"So you were just stalling," I said.

"Not *just* stalling. My offer is sincere. Your new appearance is my gift to you for walking away."

"Fine. You and the big guy walk away. Leave your prisoners with me and you've got a deal." It wasn't so much my new appearance that motivated me but the idea of facing that monster on my own while worrying about the mage sneaking up on me from behind. Saving lives was always a priority of the Daemor and in a choice between capturing graycoats or saving people, the saving always came first.

"I'm sorry but we have a quota of slaves we have to deliver. This bunch will fill that so I won't be able to do as you ask.

However, you're now faced with the choice of either getting to live and looking as lovely as you do now or staying to fight Cronk and die."

"Do you give me your word that I won't be harmed and that I will have this form forever?"

"Forever or until I die. Can't give away all of your motivation to keep me alive, now can I?"

I jabbed my sword tip into the ground and stepped towards the mage. I held out my hand.

"You'll shake on that?"

"Of course."

The mage held out his hand so I took another step forward but instead of shaking his hand, I snapped the manacles around his wrists, ensuring that his power wasn't going to be used against me. It would make it easier to fight Cronk if I didn't have to worry so much about the mage coming up behind me. Not that there weren't mages who could fight, but this one seemed too flabby to have much training.

"Foolish move, Daemor. Cronk there is a brownie." The mage could see the look of disbelief on my face. Brownies were beings who barely came up to my knee and were noted for making shoes and helping with chores. I've never seen one that came up to my waist let alone one that was twice my height. "You think you're the only one whose heart's desire was to change what they look like? Cronk had been tortured, tormented, and forced into slavery. I bought him as my personal slave then granted him in his heart's desire, creating the legendary soldier you see before you. In fact, you'd be amazed what most soldiers' hearts' desires are as they are about to enter a battle. The unit that I command has never lost a battle because of my ability to transform them. And as it happens their heart's desires typically only last as long as the battle so they transform back to their natural selves. If I were you, I'd flee because the rest of my unit should be joining us shortly. I doubt you'd survive long against just Cronk, let alone a unit of Thandua's finest Destroyers."

I have to admit that every time I'm about to get into a fight with something that looks like it could kill me I have doubts. There is a part of me that wants to run away but there's a bigger part of me that knows if I do that, evil will win. Graycoats have already taken too much from me. I wasn't going to let them take it from other people.

Besides, I fought a guerrilla campaign against the graycoats after what they did to my mother and I hurt them all by my lonesome. Now I have Daemor training to help me fight even better.

I reached up on a nearby tree and broke off a thick branch near the trunk. I lifted the mage up and hooked the chain on the branch so he dangled. No sense in letting him run off. I picked my sword out of the ground and turned to face the most colossal brownie I'd ever seen.

"Cronk, I'm leaving with the slaves so I'm giving you the choice to walk away. If you don't you and I are going to fight and you are going to lose."

That was greeted by laughter of the deep booming kind from Cronk and a much higher tone from the mage who hung from the tree.

"So be it."

My wings buzzed and I flew at his face faster than the beast could react and sliced at one of his eyes. The shock of the wound made him let go of the chains in order to bring his hand to his face. Although it would have been more helpful if he'd been an idiot and used the hand that held the battleaxe.

I'd also made a gash in the back of his head as I passed.

"You cheat! How'd you fly?"

I'm always amazed when people are shocked that I can fly. I mean I have wings and there's magic all over Faerie just for the taking.

I buzzed back but now that he knew what I could do, the

sound was enough for him to swing his axe behind him.

I barely got away in time and landed in front of him. He swung the axe towards me before I could become airborne again so I brought my forearm to block and the blow clanged off.

"You cheat again! How can your skin be axe-proof?"

I could explain to him that I was actually in full body armor but part of the charm of the Daemor badge made it look as if I was wearing an armored bikini.

No men seem to question the Daemor choice of armor but if they bothered to think about it they might. We were fighting a war. We weren't stupid enough to only armor a fraction of our bodies.

However, making it look like I was wearing next to nothing was another matter. Graycoat soldiers were almost exclusively male and they did have a tendency to be distracted by female flesh which gave us an advantage in battle.

Instead of answering, I sliced my blade at his wrist, slicing through a couple of tendons and weakening his grip on the battleaxe. I ran between his legs and dragged my sword along his heel cord, which dropped him to one knee. I flew with my sword up and used my wings to spin me as hard as they could and I swung at his neck.

I'd like to say I sliced through it on the first swing, but it's very hard to cut through such a tremendous neck in a single blow. I repeated it three more times before finally decapitating him. Cronk's head fell to the ground while his body actually took another few steps before it tumbled down as well.

I turned. The hanging mage had dropped his jaw and his skin had turned pale.

I plucked a wildflower from nearby and leapt onto the top of the giant brownie's head and plunged my sword deep into his skull. With magic can never be too careful. If his head survived, it might figure out a way to control his body. Next, I sat down on top of the huge head and took a sniff of the flower before turning to face the mage.

"Looks like you made a common graycoat blunder; you underestimated a Daemor."

"But how could you still be strong? You're so much smaller now. You shouldn't have been able to lift that sword, let take Cronk."

"You think just because my heart wanted me to look differently it wanted me to be weaker? Only a fool trades strength for beauty when she can have them both." Besides, I look more like a huge pixie now and proportionally they're even stronger than ogres.

"So, who has the keys to the chains, you or Cronk?"

"It's not going to matter for long. The rest of my unit's probably already here and just waiting for the right moment to take you out."

"Your unit? You wouldn't be talking about twenty-five graycoat soldiers, would you? With a good mix of races, all with the same Destroyer patch on the shoulder that you have?"

The mage laughed. "So you can see them. Excellent. I'll accept your surrender now."

"Why? It's not like you could give them their hearts' desired form for this battle anyway. Besides it's a little bit late for that."

"What do you mean?"

"I met up with them earlier before I found you." I got my start is a guerrilla fighter and I've only gotten better. No one, even a Daemor, engages that many trained soldiers head-on by herself. I picked them off one or two at a time. "I have to tell you that they didn't make it."

"You said twenty-five and there were thirty of them. Five of my lads hidden in the woods will be able to take care of you."

"It's cute that you think that. And I did say twenty-five but that was a low number to get you to brag and tell me how many there really were. I didn't miss any. I'm going to get you down, manacle your legs, and then you are going to tell me where the keys are so those people can be freed." Unable to run they had collapsed whimpering during the battle. Don't think poorly of them. Unless you've been where they are, you'll never understand. "Then I'll take you to Mab where you'll get a trial. And despite what you may have heard, not every graycoat gets executed."

The mage tried to shrug his shoulders but since he was dangling by them it must have hurt too much because he stopped.

"Very well. I guess you leave me with no choice."

I lifted my prisoner up so I could pull him off the limb stub but the mage had different plans. He swung the chain down behind my head and wrapped the links around my neck and pulled them tight. As soon as I felt him move, I took a deep breath. I hoped pretty me still had large lungs and strong neck muscles.

I dropped the mage and he landed on his feet. I grabbed him by the chin and scalp, then spun his head around so it was facing all the way behind him. His body went limp and dropped toward the ground but ended up hanging like a marionette from the chain that was still around my neck.

I bent down and upwrapped the links. Once freed I went back to reclaim my sword but it always ready fallen down. I guess the mage spoke the truth because Cronk was now a smaller than average decapitated brownie corpse. Since he head was no longer large enough to support my blade, it had fallen into the bloody grass. The floating mirror had also disappeared so I looked down at my body.

I was back to being thick again.

I sighed and put on a smile and went to free the slaves.

It turns out that Cronk had the keys or at least his uniform did. He was so small now you couldn't even see where his brownie size body was in the uniform. I took the sword and ran it through the mage's skull, again making sure he wasn't going to come back to life. Then I wiped off my sword on his uniform and unshackled the prisoners.

Turns out the Destroyers had laid waste to their village. I let them know that anyone who wanted to could take advantage of Mab's refugee camp. They'd be given food, clothing, and shelter. Anyone who wanted to would have a chance to join the Army and fight against the graycoats.

Or they could go and try and find themselves a new home somewhere.

Before they left, more than a few of them gave the brownie's now tiny head a kick. I didn't try to stop them. I know from experience that something like that could wind up being very therapeutic.

Beneath The Sea Of Tears

"Feeding the fish again, Terrorbelle?" Saraid said. The roane wasn't bothering to hide her laughter. The corner of her right eye crinkled up under her eye patch. I debated about tweaking the patch but worried she might push me overboard. Being half-ogre, I sink quite nicely.

"They looked hungry," I managed to say before my stomach betrayed me again by heaving what little it still carried into the water.

"I would have figured you'd have got your sea legs by now."

"My legs are fine. I need a sea stomach. Ogres don't go to sea much. Too many swim like stones," I said.

"You're only half ogre."

She was right. My pixie half gives me my wings. The ogre blood made them tough and razor sharp. "Pixies swim all right in ponds, but waves tend to overwhelm them. We haven't all been raised in underwater sea caves. And being able to turn into a seal gives you a significant advantage on a water mission. It makes sense that Mab would send you. But picking me for this mission may have been a tactical error. Not that I'm questioning orders."

Mab took me into her army, trained me. Gave me a way to get back at the soldiers who killed my mother and raped me when I was eleven. Eventually, I earned my way into the elite all-female Daemor. Not bad for a sixteen-year-old halfbreed.

Mab is the only person I'll take orders from easily.

"Mab doesn't make mistakes. Just ask her. Besides maybe the fact that you can fly and probably lift my ship over your head are factors," the roane said.

I started to say I could only get airborne for short distances and might only be able to get one end of the ship up but had to stop to make more fish food.

Saraid rolled her eyes and grabbed my hand. "Here, let me help." She pressed hard in the web between my thumb and index finger. The nausea started to lessen.

"You couldn't have done that earlier?" I said.

"If I did, you wouldn't have had a chance to bond with the native sea life. Having you landies on *Tintreach* is a chore. If your aim is off, I don't want stomach flotsam on my decks."

"Don't you mean Mab's decks?"

"Nope. Old Lightning has been mine since I was a kid. Rescued her from the man who had chopped her down and made her a ship." Sentient trees don't take kindly to that, but their slavery is common. "She came with me when I enlisted to fight Thandau." Saraid scratched at her eye patch. "He destroyed my home, killed lots of my family. Damaged my skin."

Roane and selkie are very protective of their seal skins. They've been blackmailed into marriage by people holding the skins hostage. A Roane without her skin would be as crippled as a pixie with no wings. Most of the Daemor have similar tales although Saraid told hers with more flair than most. I can't say for sure she was posing as she looked out over the sea, but she put one foot up, her right hand on her hip and the other on the sword that was strapped around her small waist. It certainly looked like she was waiting for someone to paint her portrait.

"Tintreach and I will build a new home when Thandau and his Destroyers are wiped from the face of Faerie. Until then we serve at Mab's pleasure."

And Mab's pleasure had sent us out to sea.

There are those in Faerie who consider women less than equals. Ironically, that thinking has saved many of our lives. Soldiers tend to slaughter the men and spare the women. The success of the Daemor has proved the folly of that attitude, but that doesn't mean it's been eliminated. We still have difficulty gaining allies, which is why we were heading for the underwater city of Cathair Uisce. They had managed to stay free, no small feat in these dark days.

I leaned over the side of the small ship and noticed the water was churning. "Saraid, are the fish looking for more?"

The roane looked over the bow and her face went pale. "Tintreach, move!" she screamed, drawing her sword. The ship obeyed her mistress, but it was too little too late.

Before her warning was finished, a serpentine head broke the water. It had jaws that could swallow me whole and I was no small fry. Saraid held her sword in front of her, but it was going to do as much good as a toothpick. The sea serpent lunged toward my fellow Daemor. The ship moved to protect her mistress, smacking the serpent with its hull.

I threw a bucket at the beast. "Over here, sea worm!"

The giant head snapped, locking its eyes on me. I had the monster's attention and I held no weapon. It thought I was the easier target and the tremendous jaws plunged straight at me. I dove flat on my stomach, just beneath its lower jaw. My wings shot up and bit into the soft flesh of the beast's throat. Next, I moved to my feet, careful that my wings didn't pull away from the serpent's neck as I flipped over its back. At the peak of my jump, I put my feet straight up. My weight helped my downward dive as my wings finished slicing a circle around the serpent's throat.

I landed on my hands, tucking and rolling away from the serpent's still trashing jaws. When I spun to my feet I was facing the thing. Saraid had pulled a spear from an arsenal laid out along the sides of the deck. She leapt into the air and came down spear first onto the beast's snout, skewering the wood through the entire mouth and into the deck. The monster maw was pinned shut.

The serpent was dying and trying to take us with it. The body was trashing in a last-ditch attempt to sink Tintreach, but if we removed the spear the jaws might still get us. The little ship was fighting the monster, but the struggle could go either way.

The beast's head still held on to the rest of the scaly body by the spine. My wings hadn't been long enough to cut through the bone. Only our eyes spoke as we came up with a plan. Each of us grabbed a battleaxe from the onboard arsenal and took turns chopping. My swings caused more damage, but I packed more muscle.

When only a small piece of gristle was holding the serpent together, I grabbed hold of the upper part of the spine and put my boots on the lower. I pulled and was rewarded with a snap. I landed on my rear, but the serpent's body fell over the side and into the dark depths.

There were several moments of silence, the time after battle where you realize you're still alive and the rush leaves you tired and drained. It's one of the best feelings in the world.

"And I thought a sea voyage would be dull," I said. Saraid was inspecting the damage to the deck. Given time, the ship would actually heal herself. "Think it was eating my fish food?"

"Maybe it was attracted by the schools of feeding fish who were, but I doubt it. Thandau has wizards that can control the serpents and send them out to destroy any ships that are without a protective amulet. This is the first I've encountered any in these waters. Maybe our meeting with Cathair Uisce is worrying him."

"All the more reason to get there," I said. "Want me to throw the head over and feed the bigger fish?"

Saraid grinned. "I've got a much better idea. Something that'll make Thandau's ships think twice before attacking us." She told me her plan.

"I like it," I said. Tintreach seemed to as well, as the ship was rocking playfully. "At least until it starts to rot."

The roane ran below to the galley, returning with a preservative capsule. She slapped it on the beast's forehead and the liquid quickly enveloped the thing. "The meat will keep now."

We mounted the thing on the bow, face out with the jaws propped open.

I took to the air and hovered in front. "It looks good."

Saraid stood on top of the beast's head and looked down. "It does, doesn't it?"

"Sends a message."

"Don't ckuf with me," she said.

"Most impressive," said a voice from within the waves. Below us a man floated, his torso suspended just above the water. "I trust you are the Daemor I was sent to meet?"

Saraid and I both pointed to the silver medallion with the black raven head that we each wore, then the matching emblem that flew on Tintreach's flag. The badges were traditionally worn on the chest at the point directly below a Daemor's cleavage. It helped distract some men. The underwater city's emissary appeared to be one of them.

"Anyone could just wear a raven emblem," he said.

We both laughed. "Not if they wanted to keep on living," Saraid said. Mab has a death edict against anyone who falsely claims to be a Daemor. Otherwise, it would be far too easy for the enemy to discredit us through impersonation. Keeps the Daemor assassin Daye busy. "How do we know you are who you claim to be?"

"Your Mab's messenger said I was to show you this," he said, holding up a waterproof parchment.

I dove down and plucked it out of his hand, then flew back to the deck. It held Mab's seal. "It's good."

"May I come aboard?" he said.

Saraid leapt from the head to the deck. "You may for this

visit." Tintreach was Saraid's home. Always best not to issue strangers unlimited visiting privileges. It can come back to bite you in most unpleasant places.

The waves rose in a miniature spout, lifting the man until he could walk directly onto the rail. "I am Stagnan."

"Nice trick with the waves," I said.

"I am an irragant, a water mage. There are many in my city who share my powers. It is what allows Cathair Uisce to prosper under the waves. Other than some small amounts of trade, we have remained safe because of our isolation and neutrality. Thandau's attacks on our trade ships and his attempts to find us have caused us to reevaluate that policy."

"The enemy of my enemy…" Saraid said.

"You will still have to convince King Trefor. I will bring you to my city, but there are certain conditions." Stagnan waved his hands from our heads to our boots, then pointed to a metal band on the roane's wrist. "No tracking charms."

"It's so I can find my ship," she said, leaving out that the ship could use it to find her as well.

"You will have to leave it onboard."

Saraid was not happy but complied.

The irragant handed us a strip of fabric that had suckers similar to those of a squid. "You will both put these over your eyes."

"You want us to blindfold ourselves? That is an awful lot of trust you are asking us for," I said.

"And you wish to visit the hidden city. Trusting yourselves to me only puts the pair of you at risk. By allowing you into Cathair Uisce we risk the entire city. Our location must remain unknown to all outsiders, even those who would be our allies. It is non-negotiable."

Saraid and I looked at each other.

"Sorry, then I guess our trip was wasted," I said.

"Excuse me?" Stagnan's jaw actually dropped and I had to

fight the urge to push it back up with my finger.

"With both of us blindfolded, we will be at your mercy. It is an unacceptable risk," Saraid said.

Stagnan was chewing his upper lip. "I was told to bring you."

Saraid grinned and slapped the mage on the shoulder, a gesture of familiarity his expression let us know he was not pleased with. "I have a solution. During the trip, we alternate being blindfolded. You choose the intervals we switch at and the path we take. For a mage of your obvious skills, making sure we cannot find our way back should be child's play."

"I suppose that would be acceptable," he said with a sigh.

One thing was still bothering me. "What about an air supply?"

The mage reached into his bag and pulled out a bulbous creature with a single fleshy orifice. "This should suffice."

"What am I supposed to do with that?"

"You slip the symbiote over your mouth and nose. It will create a seal and take the air you exhale and make it breathable again."

"It looks disgusting," I said.

"But efficient. Unless you can hold your breath for a few hours?" Stagnan's grin was a trifle too sadistic for my tastes when he asked that.

"Fine," I said begrudgingly.

"Just be sure not to use one for more than half a day," he said.

"Why?"

"They have a tendency to start sucking out your life force with your breath after that amount of time."

"Ckufing great," I said.

Stagnan offered one to Saraid.

"No thanks. I can handle my own air," she said. Part of the roane magic allowed them to say underwater for almost a day on a single deep breath. Saraid opened an armored and locked utility pouch on her belt. The seal skin she pulled out looked too big to have come out of such a small pocket, but she had paid a mage handsomely to have the inside made larger than the outside. The roane slipped the hide on. Slipped on didn't quite cover it. The hide had no openings. It simply parted as her body touched it, melting into her as if welcoming her home until she was transformed entirely into a seal. Except for her right arm. That stayed human from the damage Thandau's soldiers had done to her pelt. Her seal form had two eyes because her eye had been lost in human form.

"Why. . ." Stagnan said, staring at the human appendage.

I waved him to silence. "Best not to ask. Which of us gets the blindfold first?"

"The selkie."

Saraid barked at him and made an obscene hand gesture.

Stagnan looked at her. "Is there a problem?"

"She prefers roane," I said.

"Is there a difference?" he said as if answering yes would make us idiots.

It was a personal thing with Saraid. Roane are minor mages and can do much more than the average selkie, like holding their breath so long.

I didn't like Stagnan's attitude toward us and that makes me tend to give it back. "Well, if your studies haven't told you the answer to that, I'm not about to explain it."

"You seek to lecture me?"

"Nope. I seek to help broker an agreement," I said, slipping on a pair of eyeglasses Mab had given to me. They molded to the skin around my eyes and were supposed to allow me to see under water.

Next, I put the symbiote creature over my mouth and nose. It practically sucked the air right out of my lungs. I was grateful I wasn't the first one with the blindfold. The breather was bad enough. With those suckers on my face, I would have felt like someone was attacking me.

Stagnan gestured with his hand. A wave rose and stood still next to the boat. The irragant stepped out onto it. "If you two are ready to join me, I will use my powers to take you to the city. I will also protect you from the pressure of the ocean depths."

Saraid barked, saying goodbye to her ship. Tintreach moved slightly as if acknowledging the farewell. The roane then jumped overboard.

"What did she say?" the mage said, his tone demanding.

I shrugged my shoulders. "I don't speak seal."

Mab had also given me a special belt that was designed to help buoy my density. Before I had gotten onboard Tintreach, I had put it at the level that would allow me to move through the water with the same ease as a fey with no ogre blood. I hadn't had a chance to test it, so I stepped out onto the wave with more than a bit of trepidation.

The wave enveloped the three of us, pulling us beneath the surface of the water.

All my equipment seemed to be working well. Never having been this far underwater before, everything was new. Light acted differently, but when I wasn't blindfolded my glasses allowed me to view all the wonders. The only time I usually saw a fish was on a plate, so I never imaged they could move so gracefully, like dancers. I thought I was an expert in moving in three dimensions but most of the things beneath the waves had me beat. Not everything down there qualified as fish nor were they all friendly. While she was blindfolded, Saraid caught the scent of something that was stalking us. Ripping the suckers off her eyes, the roane ignored Stagnan's yelling at her to cover up choosing instead to search the sea around us. A moment later her human hand pointed at something easily the size of a full grown dragon swimming toward us. Even with the glasses, the creature was so black it was hard to see except for giant tentacles that it swam with.

My mind raced to come up with a way to fight a thing like that under the waves. Saraid raced toward me. With her small size, she could only swim with one passenger and she chose me, grabbing my hand with hers. She got us out of its path, then circled back to try to come up beneath it. Before we could try anything suicidal, Stagnan's hands glowed and the water in front of him spun like a liquid tornado. The monstrosity was caught and swirled so fast that when it stopped it couldn't even swim straight. The irragant waved his arms and the current caught the black monstrosity and smashed it into the ocean floor. It didn't move.

We swam back toward the water mage.

"Nicely done," I said, my voice muffled by both the symbiote and water.

Stagnan stared at me as if he wasn't used to getting compliments, but he managed to say "thank you."

Over the following hours, the irragant switched the blindfold between us several times over the next few hours. I was wearing it when I thought the pressure was making me hear ringing in my ears, but the sound became louder and as vibrations resounded through my body. The bells distracted me so I wasn't expecting it when Stagnan ripped the blindfold off my face, the sucker pealing nicely from the lens. From my skin, not so much. The salt water stung the hickey marks it left behind. I could hear the teasing now if they weren't gone by the time I had to report back.

We came over a seafloor hill and suddenly the city was there, huge silver towers springing out of the depths. I was expecting a small settlement. This was one of the largest cities I have ever seen. The main section was surrounded by a giant bubble filled with air. On the outskirts, there were farms with kelp and other vegetables, as well as hundreds of beds of clams and oysters being raised for food. There were several fishing parties hard at work, swimming with nets.

We were spotted as soon as we cleared the rise. A dozen armed troops came to meet us. Introductions were made. They were led by a merman named Strongfin, and had several land breathers with symbiotes. There were even a pair of selkie who began to whisper and laugh among themselves when they saw Saraid. I may not have spoken seal, but my fellow Daemor did. I didn't need to understand the words to know what was being said. Saraid's human hand opened and closed into a fist, but she remained silent.

I didn't. Two quick strokes of my wings brought me face-to-face with the merman. "Excuse me, Strongfin." I was practically shouting to make sure I was heard through the breather and ocean between us. "You are the leader of these guards?"

"Yes I am, pretty wing," the merman said, hitting on me for the benefit of his men. Things must be hard for the underwater set. I noticed his gills stopped moving when he spoke, probably using that air for the words.

"You are unable to control those under your command?" I said.

His scales darkened. "What makes you say that?"

"Those two selkie . . ." The pair did not appear offended so I assumed they were not roane. "Are mocking my companion. So either you cannot control them or you do not value their lives very highly."

The selkie both stopped and stared. The merman's head tilted in confusion.

"Saraid is a Daemor. I assume even under here you know what that means."

The merman began to look nervous. "Yes."

"Excellent. So when can we schedule the death match?"

"Excuse me?" Strongfin said. The selkie began frantically thrashing their tails.

"Her injury was earned fighting the tyrant Thandau.

They mock a badge of honor, therefore they mock *her* honor. I command this mission and I cannot let such an insult go unanswered," I said. "We'll allow enough time for them to get their personal affairs in order. We can arrange for her to fight them individually or together. I'd recommend together because after the first death, the second would be allowed to beg for her mercy. She might leave you with the one."

"I'm sure no such insult was meant," the merman said.

"Nevertheless it was given," I said, extending my wings to their fullest. It was impossible to miss the sharp edges, even underwater.

Strongfin leaned in and smiled rather weakly. "Perhaps if they apologized?"

"It would have to be a very impressive apology."

Suddenly the smile was gone, replaced with a snarl. With a single snap of his tail, Strongfin was in the seals' faces screaming at them to apologize to Saraid as if their lives depended on it. The seal soldiers saluted and swam toward the roane and proceeded to do much groveling.

"Is that acceptable?" Strongfin said.

I looked at Saraid. She looked at the two males at her feet and held their eyes. They whimpered. She turned back to me and nodded.

"I return their lives to you. I trust you will have your troops exercise more respect," I said.

"It will not be an issue," Strongfin promised.

Stagnan rolled his eyes as if he was being forced to tolerate dealing with unruly children. "If the posturing is done, can we go inside?"

The troops escorted us to the edge of the bubble, but we were a good twenty feet from the ground. Nobody seemed inclined to mention to us that we should be lower, Stagnan included. He went in first, a bridge of sea water carrying him through the wall and inside the dome. Saraid and I exchanged a look. The roane swam to me, grasped her right hand in mine. She swam us through the remainder of the water at increased speed so we hit the air moving fast. Then I took over with my wings, lowering us slowly to the ground. When we were a few feet from touching, Saraid slipped out of her skin and her human feet touched the ground. I ripped the symbiote off my face. Air never tasted so sweet. We turned to the guards that had escorted us, still on the water side. We each gave a showy bow and turned to follow Stagnan. No mention was made of his failure to warn us of the drop. Diplomacy at work.

Stagnan showed us to our rooms, perplexed by our desire to share quarters. The idiot actually asked if we were a couple, not bothering to think we did it for safety's sake. Too many people have had their throats slit when sleeping comfortably in guest quarters.

Once we were alone, Saraid spoke up. "Razorwing, thanks for earlier."

"My pleasure. I've been through it." Being half pixie, half ogre, I didn't fit in either culture, although I tried in both. I'd endured more than my share of cruelty. "I wasn't going to stand idle while it was done to you."

"The groveling was a great touch," she said. I agreed.

Our audience was scheduled for the next morning. They brought us trays of food, but we played it safe and ate the field rations we had brought with us. The bells never stopped ringing the entire night.

I took first watch, which meant I was sleeping when they came to announce it was almost time for our audience.

The palace was as impressive as any I've ever seen. Twenty armed men escorted us in under the pretense of an honor guard, but we knew we had simply made them nervous yesterday.

We were ushered right into the throne room to a standing room only crowd. On the dais were three thrones. In the center was the largest, where King Trefor sat. To his left his queen,

Gleda. The smallest throne was next over. In it sat Princess Dylane, a young woman a few years older than me.

To the king's right on the dais sat a line of mages, clothed in various shades of blue and green. Each had a whirlpool image somewhere on their person. All the royal family did as well, which indicated they were also irragants. Stagnan was third from the king. High ranking, but not top fish.

There were scores of others who could have been royalty, merchants, or party crashers.

King Trefor spoke as soon as he saw us. "Honored Daemor, please approach."

The man didn't bother with a herald. Spoke well of him. We walked until we stood at the base of the dais, then saluted by pressing our fist unto our chests where we wore the Daemor badges.

We got a half smile from Trefor, but a scowl from his wife.

"Tradition dictates bowing before royalty," Queen Gleda said.

"Tradition also rarely allows for woman warriors," I said. "Daemor bow before no one. We honor your majesties with a salute."

Gleda's scowl darkened. "I think—"

"That is acceptable," Trefor said. "You are here to discuss an alliance between the Gwragedd Annwn of Cathair Uisce and Queen Mab."

"We are, Your Majesty," Saraid said.

"What are you hoping to gain from us?" the king said.

"Troops, food, and perhaps even a safe haven to house the survivors of many of the rulings houses the tyrant has displaced," I said.

"Even if those troops are not able to be controlled and may have to be constantly challenged to death matches?" the king said with a sly grin.

"I can assure you that after a very short time in Mab's army, control will not be an issue," I said. "Nor will there be any issue of soldiers insulting visiting dignitaries or causing a diplomatic rift."

"I'm glad to hear that," Trefor said.

"What would you like from us?" Saraid said.

"Training of our own troops in Mab's fighting techniques, but done here, not on land. Escorts for our trading vessels. Favored trading status with Mab and her other allies. That is for a start."

"I think all of that is well within our power to negotiate, depending on what numbers you were thinking of for your favored status," I said.

"Excellent. There is one other matter. I would like Mab to take my daughter Dylane into her army and train her." The room filled with murmurs.

"My baby?" Gleda screamed. "I won't hear of it."

"Mother, I already told father it was fine. I would like to be a Daemor," Dylane said, sticking out her chest. If I was a male, I might be impressed.

"Becoming a Daemor is something earned, not given. I'm sure in time there is a chance of you becoming a Daemor," I said.

"I don't think you understand." The princess pointed her finger at me and it wagged with each syllable. "My father is making my being made a Daemor a condition of this alliance," Finished setting lowly me straight, she tossed her long hair over her shoulder and turned away indicating I was not even worthy to have her gaze at me.

Before I could explain that this would never be an option, the king spoke again. "Taking Dylane into the regular army will be acceptable."

"Daddy!"

"Trefor!"

The king lifted a hand for silence and got it. "The rest

of what I have to say will be done in private, between them and me. Ladies, if you will please join me." Trefor stood and motioned us toward a door behind the thrones.

One of a pair of guards who stood by the door became agitated. "Your Majesty, I must protest. To take outsiders in there alone without protection—"

"Nonsense. In there I am more powerful than any other place in the city. Ladies, please follow me."

We followed Trefor through the door. I was expected a gilded room. Instead, there was the largest spell gem I have ever seen. It was wide at the bottom, rising up much like the spires in the city and it was active. A beam of energy shot up toward an opening in the ceiling, becoming invisible before it reached the open sky of the bubble.

"Wow," I said.

"Impressive, isn't it?"

"Very," Saraid said. "This is the source of the bubble surrounding the city?"

"That and what keeps us beneath the water. Cathair Uisce is able to be moved, but when Thandau began his attacks we found the most inhospitable place in the oceans to hide ourselves."

"Then why the constant bell ringing?" I said. "It seems to announce your presence."

"To keep away the *shoryobuni*."

Saraid gasped. "Soul ships? You hid your city in the north of the Sea of Tears?"

"Very good, roane. Yes, we did. Our city cannot be reached above the waves by boat or air. The shoryobuni see to that. Of course, without the bells to drive them away, we would not be able to surface to our fleet. In fact, they would all be sunk. Each ship has a single bell which is charged from the power of the gem and allows them to ward off the soul ships. Only the captain can activate it, so even if they are taken, they cannot be used against us."

"I must confess to an ignorance of shoryobuni," I said.

Saraid smiled and slapped me on the shoulder. "Nice to hear a landie admit her ignorance. Shoryobuni are the reason even Thandau's navy is afraid of coming here. Soul ships travel through the worlds collecting spirits of the dead. Many take up residence in the north-most reaches of the Sea of Tears. Shoryobuni will sink any ship they can catch. The only way to get away is to flee while they attack another ship or to distract them with gifts. The best is a token of contradiction, a bucket without a bottom or a candle without a wick. For some reason, it confounds them. But each gift only stops one attack and they will not accept two of the same gifts during the same assault."

"And so far Thandau hasn't been willing to sacrifice the number of ships he'd lose if he tried to gain our spell gem. Not that it would do him much good. It's keyed to my bloodline, so he'd have to sacrifice most of its power to be able to use it. We have many underwater traps to prevent submerged attacks, which is why I sent Stagnan to bring you in."

"Your trust in sharing this shall be noted to Mab," Saraid said

"I believe one has to give trust to get it in return so I will also trust you with the reason why I wish Dylane to join Mab's army. My daughter has the potential to become as powerful an irragant as I and an even better ruler. Sadly, her mother has overindulged her and I have allowed it. I had assumed I would be able to undo the influence but was wrong. The next ruler of Cathair Uisce is a spoiled brat and that will spell destruction for the city I love. I have heard tales of the Daemor and I think that the training will make a woman out of her." I opened my mouth to speak, but he waved me to silence.

"I already knew that Dylane would have to earn a place as a Daemor, assuming she can. I would have it no other way. Either she will rise to the challenge or I shall have to be sure to never die. I may try anyway." In Faerie it was not uncommon to live hundreds of years, if not longer. Those with power seem to go the longer route. "Can you speak for Mab in this?"

"We can," I said.

"Excellent. Please let her know I want my daughter accorded no special treatment. In fact, Mab may have to be harder on her than those who don't assume they're entitled to be given everything on a pearl platter."

"It won't be an issue," Saraid said.

We spent the better part of the next week negotiating the finer parts of the treaty. In our off time, we began running drills with the local troops. They did well. I handled the land-based exercises and Saraid the water ones. The pair of selkie who had originally mocked Saraid took well to her training once they saw what she could do, as did the other aquatic soldiers. They soon saw the advantages of a seal having a human hand when it came to combat and weapons training.

Unfortunately, some idiot came up with the bright idea of beginning the princess's training early. That idiot's name happened to be Terrorbelle. The princess may have filled out a gown well enough to make men stare, but that hardly meant she was in good shape. Within the first twenty minutes of calisthenics she was breathing heavy and whining hard.

"I don't see why I have to do this. I'm a princess." Dylane cocked her head to one side and put both hands on her hips. Her face could only be described as pouting which may have worked on her parents but it only annoyed me. "Princesses don't fight."

"When you are on the battle line, I'm sure you can tell the enemy that and they will just give you a free pass instead of running you through."

"You don't have to be snippy about it," the princess said with a roll of her eyes and a smirk.

I wanted to wipe the expression off her face.

"You read the fine print and still signed your name on the

dotted line. It doesn't matter if you were a princess or a peasant before, soldier. From the moment the ink dried you've been a tyro, a lowly grunt who I have the poor luck to have under my command. You disobey me and I'll make your life so miserable you'll hate your mamma for not having a headache on the night you were conceived."

"You think I've going to take this sort of treatment from you? I'm going to tell Mab on you. I'm going to tell my daddy," she said, smiling as if she had won something.

"Drop and give me fifty," I said.

"And if I refuse?" she said, trying for snide. She might have pulled it off if her voice hadn't cracked. I moved my face close enough to hers that if she had inhaled instead of holding her breath the tips of our noses would have touched.

My smile was dark and I hoped scary. "I'm sure you'll be able to walk again in a week or so."

Dylane tried to outstare me but she never had to stand up to someone who wasn't subservient to her or her parent. I've been beaten, stabbed, and worse. It wasn't much of a contest. I ended it by yelling "Boo!" Dylane fell over backwards and landed on her padded rump.

I stepped forward and the princess walked backwards looking a lot like a crab with a terrified look on her face. Dylane had finally figured out this wasn't a game. I probably shouldn't have laughed at the girl's fear, but I did.

Princesses don't get laughed at. Anger joined with fear and desperation. Her hands waved, causing the water from two nearby fountains to spout up into the air. The floating pools took up position to either side of me. The penalties for attacking a Daemor were severe and usually left up to the Daemor's discretion.

My body never twitched but my wings moved faster than Dylane could follow. My upper set was at her throat and my lower at her wrists.

"That water goes anywhere but back in those fountains and I'll move some fluids of my own. Attacking a superior officer in times of war is punishable by death. Don't make me hurt you. Am I clear, Tyro Dylane?"

"Yeah," she said and the water returned to the fountains.

"That's 'yes, Daemor,'" I said.

"Yes, Daemor," she replied.

"You could have not joined." I specifically stressed that option before I let her sign. "The number is now two hundred. Get going." Princess collapsed after eight. I got in her face and she did indeed finish the two hundred pushups, whining about how much her arms hurt. I told her if I heard another complaint, she'd regret it. Sure enough, a few moments later she complained.

I took her to the palace kitchens. They were preparing a large meal and had a pile of some sort of underwater tuber. I informed the princess she now had to peal the entire lot. I told the head chef that she was to have no help and left the kitchens. I didn't go far. I had spent more than my share of time doing KP, a military tactic Mab learned during her brief exile on Earth. I knew that if left alone, a soldier will do their best to get out of it. And when I made her mop floors the day before, I caught her using her powers. I wanted to see what Princess Dylane would try this time.

A few moments later I snuck back in. Every girl in the kitchen was pealing tubers furiously. Everyone that is, except the princess who was sitting in a chair. The head chef was dotting on her, plying her favor with pastries and a cold drink.

I smiled, then put on my angry face. "What in the seven hells is happening here!" All of the girls jumped. Several dropped their knives. "All of you, move away from those vegetables, now."

The girls obeyed, but the chef put his hands on the sides of his ample belly and stormed over toward me "Now see here, this is my kitchen and I told those girls to do that."

"You did, did you?" I said.

"You have no right to be ordering the princess around," the chef said, getting up in my face. It was a mistake.

I yelled loud enough to make plates shake. "Is that so?"

I turned to the assistants. "Hear this. Every last one of you now has the day off. Anyone returning here will be locked up. Now get out!"

"Anyone who leaves is fired. And I will make sure you do not work again," said the chef. The staff stood still and the chef turned to me smirking. "As I said this is my kitchen and I am in charge here."

There was a fish on a counter that would have come up to my chin if it could stand. I stepped toward it and moved my upper wings over my shoulders. They buzzed faster than any cook could hope to move a knife. In seconds I reduced the entire thing to bite-sized pieces.

"Correction—you were in charge until you interfered with a military matter. Now everyone here answers to me. Anybody still here by the time I count five with have me personally take them into custody before their imprisonment. I'm not gentle by nature. One…" The last staffer was gone by four.

"You can't do that!" The chef's face was crimson.

"I guess you weren't paying attention because I already did it. You interfered with the training of my tyro and I can't permit that."

"I'll tell the king!"

I shrugged. "King Trefor has told me I have his full support. How do you think he will react when I tell him what you've done?"

"He'll thank me?" At my chuckle his belly didn't so much jut forward as sink down, making his head and shoulders slump.

"More likely you'll be the one fired," I said.

"I doubt he'll be happy when his noon meal is not ready in

time."

"That's your problem, not mine," I said. "And don't forget his evening dinner with all those guests."

"It's impossible. You sent away more than a dozen people. I can't do all that work myself!"

"You don't have to," I said, "You have Tyro Dylane."

"The princess?"

"No, the tyro. Have her do everything you need," I said. I leaned in close to whisper in his ear. "You don't strike me as a kind boss. You will treat my tyro the same way you would the lowest of your staff. If I even suspect you are going the slightest bit easy on her—"

I'm not a violent person by nature, but by the end of that conversation the chef was convinced I was. It took him a while, but he started ordering the princess around like she was the hired help. I stayed and made sure she did everything she was told. A couple of times the chef whispered in her ear and Dylane responded with a giggle as they tried not to look in my direction. A glare was enough to put a stop to it.

In the last hours, it looked like dinner wasn't going to be done in time so I pitched in. We made it, but barely. When it was done, Dylane was exhausted. "What now?" she said, assuming I had more for her to do, but there was already the smallest change in her.

"How do you feel?" I said.

"Tired."

"Anything else?"

Dylane looked at me confused, but her brow creased. She looked back across all the food that now was ready to serve. "Good, I guess."

I smiled. "Amazing the satisfaction a little hard work will give you. You have a dinner to attend so you best go get dressed. Hurry, you don't have much time," I said. Dylane turned to go. "One more thing, Tyro."

"Yes, Daemor?"

"You did well."

"Thank you, Daemor," she said and actually saluted me before she ran off. I waved to the chef before I left, but he glared and started chopping up something that didn't need to be cut. Odd considering everything for the meal was already prepared.

At the dinner, Dylane was seated to one side of her father, Saraid and I on the other. The queen was down the table seated next to Stagnan.

The king was very interested in his daughter's progress and asked her how things were going. The princess blanched since I was seated near enough to contradict her on any untruths.

"Well, I suppose things are going fairly," Dylane started, staring down at her plate which the chef had just put in front of her. Next came Trefor's, mine, then Saraid's. The roane started to eat, but I caught her hand and shook my head. I had a sneaking suspicion the food the chef was working on when I left was something special and unpleasant made for me.

I spoke up. "Nonsense." Dylane's pale face went crimson and she glared at me. "Your daughter did quite well today. In fact, she is in large part responsible for this feast."

"And how does preparing a meal help one become a soldier?"

"Discipline and versatility. Your daughter shows great promise. We gave the entire kitchen staff the day off and your daughter did the work of a dozen people. Not an easy task for someone who knows their way around the kitchen. Dylane did not. Which makes her accomplishment all the more impressive," I said.

"Then I shall have to try everything," said the king, smiling at his daughter whose eyes beamed at her father's obvious pride.

I offered him my plate. "Please start with mine."

The chef practically tripped over himself pulling the food away from his king.

Trefor gave him a look. "Sorry, your majesty. I brought the wrong plate for the Daemor. I'll get the correct one right away."

I picked up Saraid's plate and handed it to the chef and let my wings buzz slightly. Our eyes met and I knew we had an understanding. There would be nothing bad in the food he brought back to us.

The rest of the meal went well. It was during the after-dinner entertainment that things got interesting. There were musicians playing when Stagnan approached the king. "Majesty, might I speak to you in private for a moment?"

"Of course, Stagnan. If you will excuse me," the king said, standing. Saraid and I stood as well, sitting when the pair left to the gem room in back.

"Why didn't you tell my father about my behavior?" whispered Dylane.

"You're in Mab's army, same as us. We take care of our own. If there is a problem, we will deal with it, not go running to tattle about it," I said. The princess nodded and her head snapped toward the gem room where screams from her father had started.

The guards at the door got inside before Saraid and me, but only barely. Dylane was right on our heels. Things were bad. Trefor had been stabbed in the gut. The two guards were encased in water and couldn't move. Fortunately, they were both water breathers and wouldn't drown, but they couldn't help us either. Stagnan stood, holding the giant spell gem in his hands, a bloody dagger by his feet.

"You're too late, Daemor," Stagnan said. "Thandau will have his spell gem."

"Stagnan, it's useless to you. Only one of the bloodline can use it," Dylane said. I darted through the air toward the traitor. Saraid cradled the king and slapped a battle patch on him. It would help stop the bleeding and seal the wound until a healer could get to him.

"Oh, I found a way around that," Stagnan said, lifting one hand off the gem. It was sticky with the king's blood. "A simple spell brought his blood into my hands and bonded it there forever."

Water from the fountain rose up and swam right up to Saraid and my faces. It wrapped itself around our heads in a watery helmet, lifting us up off the floor. I had managed to take a deep breath first, but I didn't know how long it would be before I had to inhale water.

We hadn't been allowed weapons sitting so near the king, but we hadn't worried overmuch. I would have killed to have brought a table knife or even a fork with me. I could have ended the irragant with a single throw. I tried to use my wings to fly myself closer, but one wave of his hand stopped me cold.

"Let them go," the princess said, her fists balled up and her jaw clenched. Every inch of her demanded to be obeyed, but the traitor was having none of it.

"I think not," said Stagnan. "Dylane, you do not have to share their fate. Marrying you would help legitimize my claim to the throne."

"I won't consider it unless you spare my parents," she said.

"I can't leave anyone alive that could have a claim on my throne, so your parents are as good as dead. If you refuse my offer, I'll have no choice but to kill you as well. Certainly marriage to me is hardly a fate worse than death?"

There was a moment of silence and contemplation before Dylane spoke and moved toward him. "I don't want to die and I've always thought you were a handsome man, but I won't be some figurehead queen. I want real power too."

"If you are willing to go out there right now and announce our betrothal, we can discuss matters later." Stagnan extended a hand. "Agreed?"

Dylane took his hand. I can't begin to express my disappointment with the princess at that moment. It was short-lived, because her other hand reached out and grabbed the point at the top of the crystal. A moment later, the water left our heads and we tumbled to the ground.

I wheezed, gasping for air. Saraid wasn't even winded and rushed him, but he maneuvered the princess between her and him.

"You dare betray me?" Stagnan shouted, trying to put the spell gem away, but Dylane had too good a grip. She tried to pull it back but wasn't as strong as the bigger man, so she kneed him in the crotch. The mage crumbled to floor cursing. A second later pressure made my ears pop. I looked up through the open ceiling to see the entire ocean crashing down over our heads.

I flew at Stagnan, but he stood and smashed me in the head with the gem. I saw stars for a moment, but people always say I have a hard head. The spell gem split where it hit me. Stagnan got the larger piece, Dylan the smaller spire-shaped one. The traitor took the water from the fountain and enveloped himself in it before floating out the roof.

Dylane dropped to her knees, muttering a spell and clutching the fragment of the gem she was left with. I was still stunned, but Saraid pulled out the fresh symbiote that was in a pouch on my belt and put it over my face, all the while changing into her seal skin.

Moments later the water came crashing into the room, smashing me against a wall. This time my head wasn't hard enough and I blacked out.

When I came to I was still in the gem room, but I could see sky through the ceiling. The symbiote was no longer on my face. I blinked my eyes and muttered, "How?"

"Dylane raised the entire city," Saraid said, back in her human form. "Are you okay?"

"I've been better," I said, pulling myself to my feet. "You?"

"You took most of the impact. I'm fine."

"That explains why I'm extra sore. The king and Dylane?"

"Turns out the immersion in water helped him. The surgeons and healers are with him now. Dylane's over there." The roane pointed to the other side of the room.

I moved toward the princess who was pale, but conscious. "Dylane, are you all right?"

"Yes," she said, but when she tried to stand she tumbled back down. I caught her before she hit floor.

"How'd you manage to move the entire city?"

"My father has let me adjust the bubble and move the city ever since I was little. He wanted to make sure I could do it when my time came. The air rushed to the surface and there wasn't enough power to hold back the water and draw more air down so I had to raise the city," she said. "I can barely move."

"You did good. I'm proud of you," I said.

The princess practically beamed. Then I noticed the quiet.

"What happened to the bells?"

"Stagnan must have used the gem to stop them," Dylane said, trying to take some steps. She failed. Twice. "We have to stop him. Otherwise, the shoryobuni will attack and sink the city. Without an air bubble, thousands will die."

"We will, Dylane. What I need you to do is rest. We're probably going to need an irragant and with the king down, you're the strongest. I need you to rest and gather as much power as you can and be ready."

"Yes, Daemor," she said.

I couldn't help but smile. I picked up Saraid and flew toward the opening. I turned in midair.

"And Tyro, if you keep doing what you did here today, someday you will make a damn fine Daemor and an even better queen."

I headed out into the city. Wounded were everywhere. There were hundreds of bodies floating on the surface. Not all of them were dead, but the shoryobuni were closing in on the island city from all directions. The masts were made from bones and the sails looked like ragged and leathery flesh. The front of each ship had a skull whose glowing eyes cut through the dark mist that followed each like tangible shadows. I could barely make out figures on the decks, glad that mist obscured the details. I saw no weaknesses and realized I was trembling and wanted nothing more than to curl up into a ball and hide. I didn't need to feel the warmth pouring out from the protection amulet in my Daemor badge to realize dark magic was at work.

"Get me over the water. I'll gather the survivors," Saraid said.

"By yourself? Even you can't swim that fast or carry that many," I said.

"I won't be by myself. I sent for reinforcements," she said pointing to the horizon where a small ship with a sea serpent head on its bow was moving like lightning toward us.

"Is that Tintreach?"

"Yep."

"How'd you signal her? Stagnan searched you," I said.

"As a woman, not as a seal," she said. "I have amulets in both skins."

"You have bottomless buckets and wickless candles?"

"Nope, but the soul ships can't sink what they can't catch," Saraid said, pulling out her second skin. "Drop me in that open water there."

By the time I flew to where she had indicated, she was already a seal. Saraid dove out of my arms and into the water. Within moments, she had a survivor in her human hand and was swimming toward Tintreach.

I hovered, looking for Stagnan or something to use against the soul ships. The city's ships were secured to a series of floating docks. Alone, I'd never be able to get one of them sailing, let alone all of them. And without tokens of contradiction they'd only get sunk. Except I realized they traveled the Sea of Tears all the time safely and suddenly I had a plan. I dove down onto one of the ships and tore its silver bell along with its tiny belfry free from its mast, then flew back to Dylane.

"Can you activate this bell?" I said, figuring the royal bloodline could do what a ship's captain could.

"Yes," she said touching it. It began to toll of its own accord.

"Come with me. I need you to start the bells on all the ships and use them to surround the island," I said. Moments later, I had the princess on the deck of the largest ship and she had its bell ringing a second after she touched it.

Strongfin and the two selkie joined us on deck.

"Strongfin, I need you to get this to Saraid's ship," I said, holding the bell I had ripped free.

"Daemor, I must protect the princess and I do not take orders from you," the merman said.

"Excuse me, Guardsman?" the princess yelled, doing a pretty good imitation of me. "You will obey the Daemor Terrorbelle in all things. With my father unconscious, I am in charge and I turn over command of our military to her leadership. Am I clear?"

The merman bowed, practically groveling. "Yes, Princess."

"Get up," I said. "There will be plenty of time later to bow if Thandau comes to take your city. Get this bell to Daemor Saraid's ship and then obey and assist her in her rescue mission. Understood?"

"Yes, Daemor," he barked.

I handed him the bell. "Then go."

I turned to the selkie pair. "Who's faster?" The seal on the left pointed to the seal on the right. "Fine, you are to go back to the city and get enough crews for these ships. Any captains you find bring to help get the bells ringing. Then move them around the city to hold off the soul ships. Pick up any survivors along the way. Go!" I shouted. He dove overboard. I turned to the remaining seal. "You will escort the princess as she goes from ship to ship. Keep her safe or you will answer to me, understood?"

The selkie became an armed man holding a seal skin. "Yes, Daemor."

I turned to Dylane. "I'm going after Stagnan. Any suggestions where he'd be?"

"He would be with the remaining spell gem," the princess said, closing her eyes and holding the gem fragment close to her chest. "It's in there," she said, pointing to the tallest tower in the city, "the university where irrigants are trained." She looked at me. "Let me go with you. He's powerful even without the gem."

"Against one Daemor, he'll need it to even things out," I said with a bravado I didn't feel. I armed myself with three spears, an axe, as many daggers as I could stash in my uniform, and a sword from the ship's armory. "If I can't stop him, it will be up to you, Dylane. Rest as long as you can."

"Good luck," she said.

"You too," I said and took off into the sky. On the way, I fastened my water glasses and the symbiote. Stagnan would be hitting me with water-based attacks and I wanted to limit my vulnerability. My enemy had the high ground and the gem, which gave him two advantages. I was a Daemor. It had been enough in the past. Hopefully, it would be enough now.

A sneak attack was doubtful, even if I came up through the building. If he was watching, he'd know I was coming. Best to get in quick.

I wasn't fast enough. The traitor came out to greet me, kept aloft on a pool of water. I threw my first spear, followed quickly by my second. The water he commanded moved like it was a living thing, blocking both spears. Hoping to overwhelm the irragant I sent three daggers at his heart. The water deflected all three but not well enough to stop them all. The third bit into the flesh in his leg.

The irragant had stopped moving. I hadn't. Being stationary in most battles is bad, in an airborne one even more so. I used my last spear as a lance and got the mage in the side. He cried out in pain and engulfed me in water, the liquid pulling the spear from my hands. The fluid stopped me from flying. Stagnan dragged me out over open water. I started beating my wings. At first, it felt as if I was struggling through a pool of honey, but I kept at it and my wings moved faster. Slowly, I began to toss off the water, giving me more maneuverability. I got closer, planning to use the axe. Stagnan used the opportunity to put his hand on my symbiote. Suddenly it was withering and draining the air from my lungs.

Stagnan held the spell gem between his left elbow and side. I chopped the axe toward his face. He reacted as I expected, thickening the water there to stop the blade, but it was just a feint. My real attack had been to bring my feet up and kick as hard as I could. The blow knocked the gem free of his grip. A second and a third kick sent it out of the water cocoon around us, plummeting toward the ocean below. Without the extra power, he couldn't stop the next axe swing that took him at the neck. The water cocoon quickly turned red. Before I passed out, I realized we were falling, following the gem into the Sea of Tears. My watery world went black.

I woke in a bed this time. Things had gone well. The ships' bells had held off the shoryobuni and allowed Saraid and the others time to rescue the water-logged survivors. My fellow Daemor and Strongfin had recovered the spell gem after the merman had saved me. Dylane used it to restart the tower bells. The king would recover in time as would the city, with some aid from Mab.

There was no sign of Stagnan anywhere. If he survived he'd be hiding from both sides. Thandau doesn't like those who fail him.

Once Trefor was able, we left with Dylane to a heroes' sendoff. We also got commendations from Mab. Dylane got thrown into training. She told me her new commander is much nicer than me. All things considered, I can live with that.

SERVED COLD

"Your request for personal leave is denied," said Mab as she sat at the head of the long table.

I was embarrassed to admit even to myself that I had almost forgotten about the last of the graycoats that killed my mama after they ravaged us. The events of that horrible day seem a lifetime ago. If the memories weren't still so vivid in my nightmares, I'd say that the girl it happened to didn't exist anymore.

It had taken me seven years but I had found and killed all but two of the murderous bastards who stole my mama and my childhood from me. Looking back, my anger and hate would've ended up destroying me if I hadn't joined Mab's army and learned how to focus it. It fueled me but didn't have to define me.

"But Mab..."

Mab was livid when I asked for the personal time. The queen didn't want to give me leave, even after I explained what I needed it for. She only reconsidered when Kande and Daye spoke up for me. Kande is the only Daemor who knew Mab in a time on Earth when she wasn't a queen so she is not as intimidated as most of the rest of us and Mab paid special heed to her advice. The only other who isn't intimidated is Daye. I think even Mab harbors a certain fear of the Daemor's banshee assassin.

I had three days to find one of the last of the killers and get back or be AWOL. It was an Earth term Mab had adopted and the punishments for it weren't pretty and they were worse for

Daemor than they were for the enlisted.

Kande and Daye offered to come and help me, but I turned them down. Being a Daemor was about having a code of honor. What I was doing was repaying a blood debt but having someone else help me murder a man, even a stinking graycoat would not have been honorable. I just hoped that after he was dead, Mama would rest easy and my nightmares would stop.

With Mab's permission, I had placed images of the soldiers on our most wanted list. There was an artist rendition of what they looked like seven years ago. One of our informants spotted one of them, the one I called Big Ears, at the market in a small town called Oakwin. Thandau hadn't officially taken over the town, but it wasn't far from the borders of what he controlled. Big Ears was probably working as a spy in preparation for the graycoats taking the town.

I'd make sure he never passed along another report

I came out of the nearest fairy path to Oakwin at dusk and walked meekly into town in the dark.

The graycoats had descriptions of all the Daemor and a woman my size with wings and pink hair stands out even to a lazy soldier. My hair was dyed brown and tied it back in the kerchief. I wore baggy clothes to hide my wings and would be talking in monosyllables to play towards my ogre heritage. I was small for an ogre but would pass as one of the many mixed breeds that lived in Faerie.

Oakwin was a typical town with businesses lining the main road. I noted with interest that several had what appeared to be recent and rather crude fortifications made to the windows and doors. Most of the businesses were closed. I walked off the main street to one that had no torches to light it and I lifted my baggy dress up over my head and into my hands then leapt up into the sky, letting my wings take me above the streets. I wasn't exactly a stealth flyer but I wanted a quick lay of the land to make sure there were no groups of graycoats or other gangs roaming the streets with mischief on their minds. There was nothing sinister so I landed several houses down from where I took off, put my dress back on and returned to the main drag.

Oakwin was small enough to only have one tavern. And like most taverns, it was open long past the coming of the darkness.

I looked through an open window. There were plenty of what local like locals and three graycoats at a table. I couldn't tell if one of them was the man I was looking for.

I found it amusing to realize I had to suppress what had become my normal way of entering a place. I tended to strut these days. Being a Daemor had changed me for the better.

But for as long as it took to find Big Ears, I wasn't a Daemor. I was just a weary woman looking for a meal. With my head bowed and my shoulders hunched, I walked in. It may have looked as if I was staring at the ground, but I was doing anything but. I was checking the room. Big Ears wasn't here, not even among the graycoats.

Instead of taking a seat at the center of the bar, I acted like a good, little meek woman and quietly sat at a corner table

A slip of the serving girl came over to me and smiled meekly at me. "What can I get for you?"

"Bread, stew, and water." I would have preferred a steak and ale but a woman of the station I was pretending to be wouldn't have the funds for that kind of food.

"That would come to two coppers. Do you have the means to pay? I'm sorry to ask, but the owner requires me to. He's been burned too many times."

I nodded and held out the coins. The serving girl reached to take them out of my hand, but I closed my fingers. I handed her one.

"You get the other one when I get my meal. I've been burned a few times myself."

The serving girl walked over to the man behind the bar, handed him the coin. He broke off a rather chintzy slice of bread, poured some rather frightening looking stew into a chunk of wood that some people might have considered a bowl. He followed that up by pouring something brown that was what passed for water here.

The graycoats in the corner were laughing as if one of them had said the funniest thing ever heard.

"Hey sweet thing, I still need some serving so why don't you come over here and take care of what I need," said the one in the middle. He had green skin, black coarse hair and looked like he was at least part goblin. Greeny accentuated his point by thrusting his pelvis out.

The serving girl didn't go near the table and keep her head bowed. "I'm sorry, sir, but I am not on the menu."

"I'm willing to pay five coppers extra."

Not only was the goblin being vulgar, now he was just insulting. The serving girl was all jagged and pointed edges from her elbows to her ears and chin. She just started her journey into womanhood and wouldn't be done with it for a few years yet. Even an ugly woman's virginity would go for a couple of silver coins. Sadly, it wasn't uncommon for poor or cruel families to sell off their children's virginity, both the males' and the females', to make a few extra coins. When this young girl was finally of age, she could go for at least seven silvers but hopefully she had better kin than that.

The girl shook her head.

"Then you leave me no choice but to go over your head. Tavern keeper, order your wench to take care of my needs."

"I'm sorry sir, but that is not the type of establishment I run," the owner said.

Greeny pulled out two silver coins and held them between his knuckles. "Not even if I threw in this as an incentive?"

The innkeeper looked at the coins and licked his lips. It was probably as much money as he'd make in four days. He turned towards the girl as if to ask her to reconsider, but the look of shock and disgust on her face made him think better of it.

"I'm sorry, gentlemen, but no."

I found it insulting that they offered the man hundreds of times more than they offered the girl herself. It's part of why the Daemor are such an effective fighting force. Men always underestimated us.

"I've just spent months in the front lines fighting for the glory of Thandau and I will have me a woman tonight. If not the serving girl then perhaps that big girl there." Greeny stood and walked towards me. The serving girl practically ran my food to my table then fled behind the bar.

Greeny stood, towering over me. He was big for a goblin, a good three or four fingers taller than I was. "What say you, large one? Are you ready to have the adventure of a lifetime in my bed?"

"I can't say that I am."

I had only a short sword at my back, the blade to hilt barely as long as my arm from elbow to fingertip. I had a pair of daggers, one on each wrist, but I didn't want to have to use them. While normally I wouldn't mind killing a graycoat, to do so now would alert everyone in the town that there was a woman to be reckoned with here. It had been a couple of years since I'd last killed one of my former tormentors. He admitted to having been in hiding from me. Apparently, the tales of what I'd done had grown in the in the telling. It's likely that Big Ears could've heard them and he might run to ground before I found him. That didn't mean I was going to subject myself to what this graycoat wanted.

"Are your feelings hurt that I offered the little thing money and you none? You're not as comely as she, but I like a big woman. There is much more to grab onto in bed. I would be happy to give you the five coppers."

One of the graycoats laughed. "If you're paying by the pound, you need to offer her four times as much."

Greeny laughed at the joke.

"That's true. And this one is much larger in the rafters, which is a good thing, but her face is much plainer. I'd be willing to offer six coppers but that's as high as I'll go." Greeny reached down and grabbed me by the wrist and pulled me to my feet. To be honest, I let him. "You might as well take the money because I'll be getting what I want either way."

That wasn't going to happen. With my free hand, I sent my bowl of stew flying into his face and at the same time lifted my foot up to smash it down on his booted toes. I didn't hold back and heard a crunch under my heal. Greeny let go of me and I ran to the door.

"Don't let her get away and after I'm done with her, I'll be willing to share with you lot."

I ran slower than I could have. With luck, all three would follow me out of the Tavern. If the owner had any sense, he would bolt the door as soon as they were gone. That way they wouldn't come back and take out the frustrations on the serving girl.

The first part of my plan worked. Greeny's two friends ran after me as Greeny limped his way up the rear. As soon as he was out, the door slammed. Good for them.

Now I all had to do was get to a dark alley ahead of them and fly up to the rooftop. They think I'd disappeared and my cover wouldn't be blown. It might've worked too if one of Greeny's friends hadn't pulled a bolo out of a pouch and thrown it so it wrapped around my legs. As I tripped, I pulled one of the daggers from my wrist and started cutting the rope between the weighted balls. I leapt to my feet, but the two graycoats were almost upon me. A man-shaped shadow in an alley waved and whispered, "This way!"

I'm not one to normally accept invitations from strangers in dark alleys but now all three of the graycoats had broadswords pulled. Not only that, but each of them held a throwing dagger in their other hand. Even if I flew away, they might still have wounded me with a knife. With a long sword of my own or a shield, I might have had a chance. With a short sword and a dagger, I had a better chance of ending up a dead pincushion, so I ran into the shadows.

The graycoats stepped into the alley cautiously. The man in the shadows thrust forward with a long staff with a blade on the end and sliced the closest graycoat in the throat where he had no armor to protect him. As the second soldier tried to catch his comrade, the man grabbed hold of me and put my hand through a leather strap and did the same with his own.

"Hold on for your life."

He swung his blade through a thin piece of twine that anchored the other rope to the ground. Suddenly we were rushing upwards. I looked down and watched as Greeny and his remaining friend threw their daggers at us, but they clanged harmlessly against the brick wall.

The rope had pulled us to the top of the rooftop and my rescuer dropped, swung, and dropped onto the roof. Next, he reached up and took my free hand.

"Come on, we need to hurry."

He helped pull me down onto the roof and led me by the hand across the rooftop where we jumped across an alley to the next roof. We didn't slow down for several more alleys and rooftops. When we stopped, the man opened a trapdoor and led me down a ladder, allowing me to go first.

I was wary of a trap, but nothing awaited me below. My rescuer pulled a door closed behind him and slipped three bolts into place.

He brushed past me in the dark. "Follow me quietly." He opened up another door that blended in with the wall and we went down another ladder between the walls to the floor below, with him being careful to close and bolt that door behind us.

"We'll hide you here for a day or three. Those graycoats

are only visiting and shouldn't be here much longer than that. After they leave town, you can head home."

"Thank you. The rescue was very brave."

"Nonsense. I was just helping out someone in need."

"Hardly. Very few would risk so much for a stranger, especially against three graycoats. Why did you?" I asked as my rescuer fumbled on the table to find a fire stick.

"I had been drafted to fight in Thandau's army but I left. While I was one of his soldiers, I did a great many things I am ashamed of. I am trying to make up for it in some small way by helping others whenever I can."

"That is most fortunate for me." I reached in my pouch for the folded poster that had an artist's rendition of Big Ears. This guy was obviously a local and one of the good guys. Maybe he'd be able to help me find him.

He struck a fire stick and shadows danced across the room as he lit an oil lamp. "Actually, I'm trying to find someone that I heard was in this town. "

"Maybe I can help you, so long as you don't have any sinister intentions," he said with a chuckle, unable to believe that I might have might want to do someone harm. I was about to show him the paper when he turned towards me. In the lamplight, I saw his face for the first time.

I didn't need to ask my question after all. He was Big Ears.

My dagger was back in my hand I was about to wrap my fingers around his throat, tell him who I was and then end his existence when a little bundle of energy ran in and leapt into his arms yelling, "Daddy!"

"Sweet Bean! How's the best girl in the world? Besides not asleep like she supposed to be."

"Silly, you know I always wait out for you come back from helping people. Is this another lady you helped?"

My throat was desert dry. "Yes, your father helped me escape from some graycoats."

"I'm glad he helped you get away from the nasty soldiers. Graycoats killed my mommy."

I looked at him and he nodded, frowning as tears welled up in his eyes. "It's true. I was serving in Thandau's army. I was drafted as were several others from my town. We didn't fight or run because they promised that our service will protect all of the loved ones we left behind. I did it at first to protect my parents and siblings. Then later when I married, I stayed in the army so my wife could live in a protected town. Then I stayed in longer so my daughter could grow up safe. Then one of the other guys who enlisted with me deserted and the dark one decided to punish him by having troops raze our town. They killed and did worse things to my wife. Things I had done to others. When I heard about it, I ran as fast as I could home but my parents, my siblings, everyone in this town had been killed, everyone except my little sweet Bean here." Big Ears mussed his daughter's hair.

That seemed suspicious to me. "How did you survive, little one?"

"My mama knew the soldiers were coming so she hid me in our manure pot, deep enough so just my nostrils stuck out and she covered them with some straw. Then mama tried to hide too but they found her. She made me promise not to come out no matter what. I kept my promise and I didn't even come out when I heard everything they did to her."

"You were very brave and smart to listen to your mother," I said.

Bean nodded. "That's why I want all the graycoats dead."

I got down on one knee and looked the little girl in her eyes. I put my hand on her shoulder, after first placing my dagger back in its wrist sheath. "I understand. Graycoats took my mother from me too, only I didn't get away unhurt." Big Ears was scrutinizing my face and then looked down to where a corner of one of my wings stuck out from beneath the dress and realized who I was.

"Sweet Bean, why don't you get to bed while I get this nice lady situated for the night."

"Okay. What your name, lady?"

"A lot of my friends call me Razorwing.

"Well Razorwing, you make sure you watch out for those graycoats and kill any who try to hurt you."

"I will."

Once the little girl was out of the room, Big Ears turned to me, his face sad but the rest of him standing like a soldier on review. "You're here to kill me, aren't you?"

"Yes."

Big Ears nodded. "I had heard about how you had gotten some of the others."

"You are the second to last to have escaped me."

Big Ears nodded. "What we did to you and your mother is inexcusable. I regret it. I'm very sorry for what we did. I would offer you an apology here and now but it would only ring hollow to your ears."

"So now you want to apologize? Do you think saying you are sorry will stop me from killing you for what you did?"

"I don't."

"Damn right. I'm not that scared little girl anymore. I am a Daemor and I could kill you six ways before you could reach your blade."

Before I could blink, his sword was in his hands and pointed towards me. Ckuf. I was an idiot, talking when I should've been killing. Now my poor mama will never be fully avenged.

"Now I suppose you're going to tell me that you are a changed man. Tell me that you're different than you were then as you run me through." I said.

Big Ears gave a chuckle. "I'm not going to run you through." He tossed the sword aside onto the floor. "I've hurt you. And I'm not going to tell you I'm a different man. I'm the same man, just making better decisions. Sometimes I wake up screaming from nightmares. I see your face and your mother's as I relive what we did to you as the others take their turn. Then your face changes to that of my daughter. Trust me, I truly realize what I did was horrible."

"Then why did you do it?"

Big Ears paused to consider his answer. "In this world, those with power hurt those without. They put us in the uniforms and give us weapons and sent us out to fight. For the first time in our lives, *we* had power. I guess we thought we would get back at the world for what it had done to us. I won't waste your time telling you what abuses I'd suffered before that day because the worst of them pale in comparison to what I helped do to you. It was mob mentality. We had been taught that taking women's virtue was one of the benefits of being a soldier. That it was our right as victors in a battle. I think it was supposed to motivate us. Being a soldier is alternating boredom with absolute terror. Doing those horrendous acts was a release of the stress and an affirmation of power."

"What you did to me was not a release. It was an attack of the darkest sort. You complain you have the occasional nightmare? I have nightmares every night and it takes every bit of my self-control not to wake screaming each time I sleep."

Big Ears actually had tears streaming down his face.

"How dare you cry just because you're about to die. Do you think your tears will stay my hand?" This time I was smart enough to pull the long dagger from out from underneath my dress.

"I'm not crying because I'm scared of dying. I'm crying because I'm thinking of you as someone's daughter and realizing no matter how hard I try, I can never make up for what I did that day. You have every right to kill me and I won't make a move to stop you. I ask you to have mercy on my daughter. She is innocent. I should be punished but I ask you to spare her life."

The door swung open and little Bean bounded in her nightclothes and wrapped her arms around her father's waist. I hid the dagger from the child.

Big Ears bent down, picked his daughter up and hugged her hard.

"Sweet Bean, you know I love you and that you mean the world to me, don't you?"

The girl giggled. "Of course, I do Daddy. Don't forget tomorrow, you promised to play blind ogre's bluff with me."

Big Ears looked at me over the girl's shoulders, his eyes full of devastation, straining to look happy instead of tear up. "I remember."

The former graycoat put his daughter down and Bean turned to me.

"Maybe Razorwing can play with us."

I fumbled for words. "Well, maybe. We'll see I guess."

The girl hugged me and I put the hand that didn't have the blade around her back and squeezed.

We were both silent for several seconds after the door closed behind her.

"Although I have no right to ask anything of you I will anyway. If when you kill me, you would not mutilate my body or my face. My little one will likely be the one who finds my corpse and I don't want that to be her last memory of her father."

"Fine." I didn't want to cause that little girl any more pain than her father's death was already going to.

"I'll give you a moment to make peace with whatever higher powers you believe in."

Mab would have been critical of that act of mercy and as I watched, Big Ears reached behind his back and pulled a throwing dagger.

I realized too late that Mab would have been right yet again as I brought up my blade to block his, but he was too fast. I turned so my shoulder would take the impact instead of my chest and then realized I hadn't been hit.

There was a grunt behind me. I turned to see Greeny with his sword drawn. He'd come through the same tunnels we had. The dagger had lodged in his throat.

The graycoat soldier fell to the ground and bled out.

"Why did you do that? If you'd waited a moment, he would've killed me. You could have killed him then and lived."

"Thanks to my nightmares, I'm used to seeing my daughter's face replace yours. I couldn't let him kill you. I owed you more than that. I owed you a life to live."

"You know this doesn't change a thing, right?" I said.

Big Ears nodded. "I do."

I sighed and pulled back my blade so I could stab into his stomach and up into the heart. His death would be quick. Then I would lay him out in fresh clothes and clean up his blood so Bean wouldn't have to see her father like that.

Big Ears closed his eyes when I placed the point of my blade against his stomach. As I willed my hand to move the blade forward, I found I couldn't move. No, I wouldn't.

When he realized he wasn't dead, Big Ears opened his eyes and watched me tuck the long dagger back under my dress.

"You didn't kill me."

I shook my head. "I have every right to, but your death would serve no other purpose other than to quench my rage. You are doing your best to raise your daughter and to fight back against the graycoats. You're saving lives. If I kill you, I am as good as killing those who you would save."

"So you forgive me?"

"Oh no. I don't know if I can never do that, but perhaps you may be the one of my attackers I can grow not to hate."

Big Ears dared a small smile. "I can live with that."

"You can live with it as long as I allow it. If I find that you turned back to your graycoat ways or hurt that girl in any way,

I will return to end you. You won't even see me coming. Are we clear?"

"Yes."

"I will arrange for someone from Mab's army to contact you to coordinate your resistance. You'll know them because they will tell you that they bring Razorwing's mercy. Welcome to Mab's resistance."

"Thank you. I will do as you ask."

What followed was a long and awkward staring contest. Big Ears broke away first.

"I best be on my way."

"Bean will be upset if you're not here she wakes."

"She should be happy enough that she still has her father."

I took off my outer dress to reveal my armor and my wings flexed into their full position. I opened the window and looked out into the night sky.

I don't remember exactly how I got back to Mab's castle, only that my mind was still trying to adjust to what had just happened.

THE LESSOR

"Why do these things keep happening to me?" I said, waving my sword back and forth in frustration.

I stopped once I noticed the blood flinging about the dungeon. I didn't want any of it spattering into the spell circle. I wasn't sure if that would free the demon, but that was one chance I wasn't about to take.

"Just lucky, I suppose," said the grinning crimson demon. "Your own fault really."

"How the hells do you figure that?"

The demon's smile widened at my choice of words. "You didn't have to kill Kaldon. You could have wounded him. Or at least attacked from the front. Very unsporting of you."

The last thing I wanted was to get in a debate with a thing from the Pit, but until I figured out what to do with what was very obviously a him, I didn't have any better ideas. "I suppose he was summoning you to get a report on the weather."

"Bright and bloody, with a hundred percent chance of slaughter," said the demon. "Of course, I can tell you if your fellow Daemor will take the castle or die in the attempt. Not all of them were able to fly above it to sneak in like yourself."

"We'll win," I said, dragging the mage's corpse to the far end of the chamber before I wiped the blood from my sword on his robe.

"Ah, confidence. Very inspiring and believable coming from such a lovely lass," he said in what I imagined was his bedroom voice. If I closed my eyes, I might be able to consider it sexy, but with my eyes open I had trouble getting past the scales and horns. Not that scales and horns are bad in and of themselves, just when attached to a demon.

It was my turn to laugh. My half-ogre parentage made sure I didn't receive many sincere compliments on my beauty.

"You find your beauty amusing?" he asked, leaning forward in the same manner a certain kind of man does in a pub when trying to convince a woman he is something he's not.

"No, but it is hard to believe in your sincerity after that phony piece of flattery," I said, looking around the room and seeing nothing of use. I guess it was too much to hope for a manual on how to send this thing back to Hell.

"Insecurities, at such a delicate age."

"Hey, I'm nineteen," I snapped and instantly regretted it. I'm one of the youngest Daemor and it's a touchy subject. For an ogre, this would be my first year as an adult. For my pixie half, it would be my fifth.

"You are a very mature lady for such few years. And beautiful, although it is sad that you cannot see what is so obvious to me," he said, pushing his lips together and moving his head side to side in a slow and calculated motion.

"Perhaps you need glasses," I said.

The demon's eyebrows rose at that. "You've spent time on Earth."

"No, but some of the other Daemor have," I said as I flipped through papers piled on a stone table.

"They left beautiful Faerie? Not something I'd do."

"Faerie is in the midst of a bloody war in case you haven't noticed," I said.

"I am quite aware, which is exactly my point, although I suppose beauty is in the eye of the beholder. From my perspective, you are beautiful, especially those wings. They look sharp enough to decapitate."

They were, but it was none of his business so I kept looking for a way to get rid of him.

"You won't find anything. Kaldon was meticulous, memorized everything."

"You'll understand if I don't take your word for it," I said, turning the table on its side in hope of finding some hidden instruction.

"Suit yourself. I'm not going anywhere."

"We'll see about that," I said, but it seemed hopeless. Magic helped people in Faerie speak and understand each other, but it didn't work the same for the printed word. I couldn't make horns or wings of the papers I was rifling through. I was good at fighting and breaking things. I certainly wasn't a mage. All I knew about demon summoning was to avoid it. Sadly, that wasn't an option.

"What is your name?" the demon asked.

It's Terrorbelle, but I wasn't dumb enough to tell him that. I shot him a look instead. "What's yours?"

"Very nice, but you can't blame a guy for trying. This doesn't have to be a losing situation for you," said the demon.

"Really?" I said, not bothering to disguise the sarcasm in my voice.

"Kaldon has already completed the binding. I'm at your mercy. I am bound to perform whatever task is set before me."

"Sorry, I'm not ready to part with my soul," I said.

More laughter. I guess I should consider giving up the front lines to entertain the troops. If Hornhead here was any judge, I was hilarious. "That is one price. Life and blood is another."

"I'm not willing to offer up innocents to you either," I said.

"Who said anything about them having to be innocents? Send me to do your bidding, kill your enemies for you. Their lives, their blood could suffice as payment. As long as you offer at least one up to me of your own accord," he said. "Isn't there anyone you'd like to see dead?"

I stopped my searching. There was. More than just one. It must have shown on my face.

The demon wrinkled his brow. "Let us see who a gentlewoman like yourself would want slain. Your fellow warriors, who steal your glory?" The demon rested his pointed chin on the back of his scaled hand. "No, glory does not attract you. But you do have issues with physical attractiveness. I could make you beautiful."

It was my turn to laugh. "I thought I was already beautiful."

Hornhead smiled and nodded approvingly. "Very good. You are to others, but not to yourself, so in your mind you are not attractive. I could change that."

"By messing with my mind?" I said, tossing through shelves full of books.

"No, just your body," said the demon.

"You're not going near my body, demon. I've never been that desperate." The one time my body was changed was done without my leave.

"You wound me and I've been nothing but nice to you, Daemor," pouted Hornhead.

"I'm not exactly in the mood to apologize," I replied as I reached up and pulled down the bookcase. There was nothing behind it but wall.

"Nor should you be. I wouldn't have to touch you to make you the most attractive woman on the face of Faerie," he said.

"I could save up and buy a glamour. What do I need you for?" I said, though I've had my fill of glamours too.

"A glamour merely changes what others perceive and they are hardly foolproof," said Hornhead. I couldn't argue with him on that point. "What I offer is to change you and perhaps then you could begin to change yourself."

"I have enough trouble dealing with Mab's mind healers. I don't need more problems from you," I said, patting down the stones in the walls in hopes of finding some secret chamber.

"We will forget about beauty then. What of power? I could make you the rebel queen instead of Mab. You could lead the troops, make the crucial calls, save the day," said the demon, rubbing his hands together.

"No thanks. Too much work," I said. Besides, it was way too much responsibility.

"How about physical power? I could make you indestructible and stronger than any foe," promised Hornhead.

I was already pretty strong, although it would be nice to not have to worry about getting killed. "Nah, life would be pretty boring then."

"Then a mystic weapon. A magic sword or shield perhaps?"

"Probably wouldn't match my outfit," I said.

Hornhead chuckled. "I see I am getting closer."

"You get close to me, buster, and I'll beat you down," I said, getting on hands and knees to search the floor.

"There is no need to bow to worship me, not that I'm not flattered," said Hornhead.

"Dream on," I said.

"I'll have you know that there are succubi who beg for me," said Hornhead, pushing his pelvis forward so his demonhood was made more prominent.

"To what? Leave them alone?" I said. I sat near the pile of books and started flipping through pages.

"Mortal and gentry women have been known to scream my name."

"What, during nightmares?" I asked, tossing another book aside. My comments seemed to annoy Hornhead.

"Don't strain your eyes. Light another candle," said the demon. The only light in the room was coming from a lone black candle on the front tip of the spell circle that was keeping him trapped.

"I'm good," I said. "I can see well enough."

Hornhead seemed disappointed by my answer. "I have something else you might be interested in. Love."

"You're not my type," I said, picking up another book.

A masculine giggle came from the demon's mouth. "Not me. The most handsome man in the world could be made to fall in love with you. And you with him, if you like."

Hornhead was playing dirty. Like any girl I dreamed of finding my true love, but how I looked made that more challenging. "So you would enthrall some gorgeous guy to fall in love with me?"

"In essence. You could do no wrong. He would protect you with his very life and fill your nights with passion," said Hornhead.

But it would never be real, only a spell. "No thanks."

"Wealth and treasure?"

"Wouldn't have enough time to spend it," I countered.

"You are a challenge, aren't you? I need to look deeper to find your price. Everyone has theirs, you know," said the demon, staring at me in silence. It was far more uncomfortable than his trying to tempt me. "I've got it. I will deliver to you those remaining men who slaughtered your mother and did horrible, unspeakable things to you when you were but a child."

"Get out of my head," I demanded, barely stopping myself from flinging a book at him. Crossing a spell circle was a bad thing, especially with a demon on the other side.

"Not that it isn't a wonderful place to visit, I'm sure, but I have other methods of getting information. You have yet to find the last of your attackers and avenge yourself. I could gather him for you, even if another has stolen your chance at vengeance by killing him first. We could place his head on a spike surrounding your mother's resting place in tribute to her."

"No thanks. Ma always liked flowers and jewelry," I said. Not that she was above wearing skulls for a belt, but they were from animals, not people. Still, there was no denying the temptation, but how to do it while avoiding the damnation was beyond me.

"Then what of Thandau?" That stopped me short and I

rose to face the demon. "That got your attention, didn't it? The despot you and your fellow women warriors are toiling so hard to defeat. The creature your attackers were in service to. I could destroy him for you. You only need ask and grant me some small favor."

"Which is?"

"Break the spell circle. Obliterate some small portion of it and grant me freedom."

"And trade one tyrant for another? I think not," I said.

"I would, of course, grant you my personal protection in perpetuity."

"Just how would I be able to enforce that if you changed your mind?" I said.

"Standard contract. Spell out what it is you want and sign in blood," said Hornhead.

"I am not letting a demon lose," I said.

"Ah, but you are not rejecting the deal outrigh,t are you?" he said.

The chance to destroy the enslaver and slaughterer of Faerie? Entire cities have been slain by his forces. I've seen corpses piled to the sky. What would it be worth to stop that? My voice was barely a whisper when I answered, "No."

"Excellent. I can work with that," said Hornhead, but I noticed him staring out of the corner of his crimson eyes at the black candle. It was burnt down to a nub. "I can understand your position. You're not a bad person and you don't want to be responsible for the killings of innocents. And that is exactly what I would end up doing too. So we put a clause in that I cannot kill without your express permission."

"What about maiming?" I asked.

The demon shook his head. "Not going to let me have any fun, are you? We can put that in there too. Shouldn't you be writing this down?" The demon was again trying to not look at the black candle. "There is blank parchment and quills on the table."

I walked over and picked it up. "Just because I'm writing this down, doesn't mean we have a deal yet."

"Of course not. It becomes binding once your blood is on the parchment," said Hornhead.

"And what would be expected of me?" I asked.

"Allow me one kill a year. The victim would be of your choosing. You may pick the most evil and heinous people and I will eliminate them for you, starting with the tyrant."

"What if I refuse to give you a target one year?" I said.

"It would be most unfortunate. I would have to take your life. And soul. But that need never happen," said the demon.

"Why not?" I asked.

"Because there are so many wicked in the world, you will never run out of people deserving of death," said the demon.

"And what do you get out of it?" I said.

"Oh that. Not much. I get to stay in Faerie and not return to Hell. That's enough motivation, trust me," said Hornhead.

"I don't, Hornhead," I said.

"I don't see why you had to go to name calling. You don't see me referring to you as Razorwings, do you? But you don't have to trust me; you just have to spell everything out in that contract. You can also have me kill in between if you like. I don't mind and I get bored easily."

"That's good to know. What happens if I die?" I asked.

"Won't happen. I won't let it, because when you go, I go. So do we have a deal?"

I held the paper out in front of me, reading what I wrote. "I don't know. I have to think about this." It wasn't like I hadn't killed before, but it was always someone trying to kill me. Even this mage Kaldon. Sure I snuck up on him, but had he loosed this demon, Hornhead would have slaughtered myself and the rest of the Daemor as we attacked this castle.

The black candle started to flicker and Hornhead started

to panic. "Please sign. I'll even put in a clause allowing you a onetime renegotiation before the second victim."

"That's awful generous of you. Too generous," I said, my suspicions growing.

Hornhead started to scream and his entire body swelled up to an enormous size. Flames filled the spell circle and focused into a tiny beam that shot out onto the tip of my left index finger.

"Ow," I said. The tip of my finger was dripping blood. "What are you doing? I thought a demon couldn't harm anyone outside of a spell circle?"

Hornhead had collapsed to the floor and was gasping for breath. He was now half the size he had started at. "Normally, we can't. There is a tiny defect in Kaldon's circle. Not enough for me to gain freedom, but enough for me to affect the world outside if I am willing to spend the power."

"Why do it?" I asked.

"Hell is not a place most want to be, not even demons. I don't want to go back. Please, press your finger on the paper and seal the pact with your blood." The black candle flickered again. The wick was almost burned through.

"I'm still not sure," I said.

"We haven't time to waste," said Hornhead. "You know very well that Mab would want you to do this. In fact, she would order you to."

I put the paper done at my side. "Be that as it may, I'm not going to be pressured into this."

Hornhead wouldn't even look at me. He had eyes only for the dying flame on the shrinking wick. "Okay, take your time, but you will have to call me back."

"I have no idea how to do that," I said.

"It's simple. Kaldon already did the hard work. Simply soak a wick in a drop of your blood and reuse this very wax to make another candle. Light it and say my name three times to summon me. Use the same spell circle if it would make you feel safer."

"I don't know your name," I said.

Hornhead must really have been desperate because he told me what it was. "I am Ghordon. Don't forget. Please, don't forget…"

Then the candle went out and Ghordon screamed. I drew my sword, ready to defend myself, but there was no need. The demon was actually gone and I was left standing next to a pile of wicks on Kaldon's workbench with a bleeding finger.

As I listened to the screams of the dying and wounded outside, I was left to decide which was the lesser of two evils—and what I was going to do about it.

Bonus Stories!

THE SWORDS OF THE DAEMOR

IT WAS FAERIE'S DARKEST HOUR WHEN
THANDAU RULED THE LAND.
POWERS GREAT AND SMALL FLED, HID,
OR BOWED TO THE TYRANT.
BUT THERE WERE SOME
WHO DARED TO FIGHT BACK.
THE GREATEST OF THOSE WERE THE
DAEMOR,
FEMALE WARRIORS,
THE ELITE OF MAB'S REBEL ARMY.
THEY RISKED ALL SO THAT FAERIE
WOULD ONE DAY AGAIN BE FREE.
THESE ARE THEIR STORIES.

SPOILS OF THE DAYE

A Tale of Daye the Deadly

Young and old stood together waiting. Waiting for the enemy to arrive. The women had spent the last few hours stacking stones by the roadside in anticipation. No man, save children or the decrepit, was present. Any male able to carry a spear had one thrust into his hands as he was put into military service. Both armies were just as guilty of this.

The graycoats had killed my husband and my babies. I was on my way to join Mab's rebel army to see if they had use for a banshee. Maybe I could bring some death down upon those who killed my family instead of only seeing it coming. Although the gift never works to give warning for those we love or I would have saved my lovelies somehow.

Thandau himself stayed tucked safely away in his fortress in the capital, far away. Two days march due west of this sleepy village lay the front. Thanks to the village's location, the prisoners from Thandau's army taken at the Battle of Tarch were on their way to a trial and possible execution at Mab's court by way of the main thoroughfare.

The streets lay quiet with the men off at war. Like too many places, the women kept the village running smoothly as each wife took up her husband's profession and the children performed the mothers' jobs. Most I spoke to admitted that the town was in better shape now than it had been in years. Regardless, the women would willingly endure chaos if it would allow their loved ones to be at their sides.

The last harvest had been bountiful but much of the food was ordered sent to the troops. The civilian population was put on a weekly ration of food, more than enough to provide nourishment, but the villagers felt in that a choice between the warring factions, Mab's was, if not the better, at least the safer. The rebel queen never slaughtered a town or innocents. Thandau could not make that claim, many times over.

Sustenance was not the only hardship that loomed on the horizon. A slight chill filled the autumn air, a grim promise of the winter yet to come. Thoughts of their husbands, sons, and brothers' homecoming when the war was done kept their hearts and souls warm.

For me, it would be a very cold winter indeed. My first alone in years. My lovelies were buried in unmarked graves to prevent desecration by the graycoats. All I have left are my memories and a few letters.

I do have something else to remember my husband. Shortly before he was slain, he'd spent a small fortune on a heeda, a thought stone. The elements in the stone were sensitive to thought and emotions. A heeda held a short message indefinitely. The stones could be used again but that wiped away the preceding message. I would never do that. The heeda was the only piece of my husband I had left. It held the last words I'll ever hear from him.

I carried the stone in a pocket close to my heart. Several times a day I reach in and touch the stone and hear his thoughts – *Daye, I love you. Now and forever.* I can feel the emotion with he had recorded the message. The heeda is all that keeps me going.

Before the tragedy that forever changed my life, I used my meager savings and whatever I could beg or borrow to buy a second stone for my husband. I planned to give it to him on our next anniversary. He and our twin girls were taken just a week too soon for that to happen.

I lay in bed for a week but eventually dragged myself out. One of my family, my oldest son, Jonny boy, survived only because he was away fighting in Mab's army. I decided to record a message and send my love to Jonny with the second heeda. The next day, less than a week after the slaughter of the rest of my family, one of Mab's couriers brought me the last letter my Jonny had written. The courier also had the sad duty of informing me that Jonny was dead, buried where he fell on the battlefield. I sunk back into my grief, much deeper than before. He was the last of my family. I was left alone in the world.

The second stone lay unused in a deep pocket. I've never been able to bring myself to sell it, even though I need the money badly.

I stared off into the faraway grey of the sky and felt a rumble deep in my gut. Hunger gnawed at me. I only had half a loaf of bread and a single sausage left. If I wasn't accepted into the army, I might starve. No matter how hungry I get, I am determined to make this food last. I am strong. I will endure.

The trees on the roadside were quickly being stripped bare as the local women sharpened their aim. With each toss, bits of bark flew into the air. I joined in, imagining the wood to be pieces of enemy flesh, each throw a vengeance for the loss of my loved ones. I will make a graycoat pay with blood for my blood. That would start to right the wrong.

In the distance, columns appeared. In the lead were Mab's officers on horseback, proudly displaying their medals and clean uniforms. Each had a sword which was waved in the air as if at an invisible enemy. They reminded me of strutting peacocks. There were no Daemor with them. Foot soldiers flanked the sides of the parade, eyes facing front, almost afraid to look anywhere except at the back of the head of the soldier in front of them. I wonder what the first man in each line does.

When they entered the village, a huge cheer rose from the assembled women. I may have yelled the loudest.

"Where are the graycoat bastards?" cried one woman, shaking a rock-filled hand above her head.

"A perversion of all that is right is what they are," said another.

"I just want to make them pay for my family," I said as the icy fingers of bitterness tightened their grip around my heart. I fear my compassion was as much a causality of war as my lovelies.

The first graycoat in the procession, bound hand and foot in chains, was the hated General Helvam. He was covered head to toe with bruises and blood dripped from multiple open wounds on his body. The tip of his left ear had been torn away. This was not the first village he was dragged through nor would it be the last. It would be a miracle for him to survive long enough to reach the Mab so the queen could put him to death.

The graycoat general's head was hung low and both eyes were nearly swollen shut. The sight of him filled my heart with a cruel joy. As soon as he was within range, he was greeted by a barrage of stones. Helvam fell to the ground whimpering and blubbering. It took three soldiers to drag him to his feet amidst the jeers of the crowd. Finally, an officer – a lokhagos or captain – reluctantly asked the ladies to save some stones for the other prisoners. I threw a final stone which struck him in his head. Helvam would have fallen to the ground if it had not been for the arms which already held him up. The lokhagos turned to scowl at me. I simply smiled back, shrugged my shoulders and held up two empty hands. The officer continued on.

The next to arrive were Helvam's officers. Each received the same warm welcome their leader had gotten. Some cried, some moaned, while two officers impressed the crowd by holding their heads up high and made no sound or indication of pain, despite the many projectiles they were bombarded with.

Pulling up the rear, in the exact opposite order observed during battle, was the graycoat infantry. One of the infantry, weak from hunger and abuse, collapsed. Almost immediately Mab's foot soldiers were upon him, striking his back with the blunt end of their swords and spears, ordering him back on his feet. From further ahead in the procession three graycoats ran back to aid their fallen comrade, blocking the blows meant for his body with their own. They gently helped him to his feet and carried him forward.

I admit, such a showing of compassion and courage by graycoats stunned me. For a moment, I wasn't truly sure who stood before me. A memory called to me from the past. Of my neighbors' two boys carrying my son home after he fell out of a tree they were playing in.

For the first time, I truly looked at the young graycoats before me and my vision saw beyond their uniforms, past the rhetoric, past the propaganda. In a flash, they were no longer a faceless enemy but people. I pointed a finger toward one of the three who had run back.

"Why he's no older than my Jonny was. He's just a child. Another mother's son."

At my words, the crowd fell silent and we stared at the children before us. Not a single stone flew. The other women saw the foot soldiers as I had. As someone else's husbands, sons, and brothers. Hatred wavered as guilt flowed in to take its place. Helplessness enthralled us and held us tightly in its grip.

I was the first to break the silence and defy helplessness.

"I won't be the cause of harm to another woman's son!" The throwing stone fell out of my now limp hand to land harmlessly in the dirt. Other stones from other hands soon followed. It was not enough.

My soul filled with anguish for the plight of the poor boys before me. The lads were on their way to the gallows. They would not survive the week.

Without thinking, I ran out into the street to the side of the graycoat who reminded me of my Jonny boy. The other women stared at me wide-eyed. I sprinted so swiftly that no foot soldier moved to stop me.

"Here." I pressed a sausage and half a loaf of bread into the young soldier's slim hands. He grabbed my hand in thanks as he began to share the food with the injured graycoat.

Inspired, acting almost as one, the other women poured out into the street, each adopting a boy to give a little food and drink to. The graycoats each smiled their thanks as their eyes widened in disbelief.

Amidst the confusion, the foot soldiers tried to restore order. I quickly took something out of a deep pocket and handed it to "my" graycoat and whispered in his ear. The boy nodded then closed his eyes and frowned his brow in concentration. When he was finished he handed it back to me and whispered in my ear. I nodded and ran back to the roadside just as the Lokhagos came back to see what the disturbance was about. We women quickly dispersed as the graycoats hid their gifts under torn clothing. The officer ordered the march to begin again. It did, a fraction less morbidly this time.

We women stood, watching until the prisoners marched out of sight. The others returned to work. There was a war on after all and much work to be done.

As I walked away, a smile crept up slowly on my face. My thoughts were of another mother who would have a heeda stone with a last message from her son to comfort her in her time of grief.

And the icy fingers of bitterness around my heart finally began to thaw.

LUCKY DAYE

A Tale of Daye the Deadly

Sometimes you just get lucky, but it's not always of the good variety. There had been rumors circulating for a while that some woman was impersonating a Daemor. Very bad move on her part. Mab is fighting a losing guerilla war against Thandu's forces to free Faerie from the tyrant. One of the strongest things she has going for her is the reputation of her troops, especially the Daemor. We're the elite, the best of the best. And we're all women. Mab's got some serious issues, but then I can't talk. I'm a banshee that kills people, which is not exactly a traditional role for a caoineag. A Bean Sidhe is supposed to warn of the dark embrace, not hasten it. It's made me an outsider among my own people. My given name is Daye, but I've heard them call me Dark Daye or Daye the Deadly in frightened whispers. Most are too afraid to call me that to my face.

Mab has a death edict against anyone impersonating a Daemor. If the people can't trust us, then we have no hope of victory. I get to enforce her orders.

Lucky me.

Taking care of impersonators occupies a good piece of my time. Not that there have been that many after the first dozen; most of those, Mab punished herself. Very old school, as Kande—a human Daemor—likes to say. Even though they are few in number, they don't exactly walk up to me and say "Kill me." Finding someone in Faerie can be a tremendous task.

I can't say I don't like my work, mainly because I get to kill the bad and I'm considered exceptional at what I do. If my job helps me work out some anger issues, it's a bonus.

A rule of thumb for an assassin: Never go in blind. Know your prey, a good trick when all you have to hunt are rumors. I typically travel incognito and I strive very hard not to repeat disguises. The locals aren't stupid. They talk about anybody new in town. If a certain type of person were to regularly show up right before a killing, gossip would eventually get me caught when I showed up somewhere. The price Thandau has on the head of any Daemor is sizeable. The bounty on Mab is enough to buy a small kingdom. The reward for my capture is almost as high.

There is one cover identity that I have repeated time and time again: that of a widow. There are too many of them of late. Thandau forcibly drafts the able-bodied males. Many don't return, which leaves a small population imbalance. Probably the most practical reason for Mab's recruiting choice.

A lot of rural widows come into town to get drunk when they get the news. Normally, they're too busy out on the farm to bother. With the current state of affairs in Faerie, nobody even notices a new widow. There's another one almost every day.

Besides, I like wearing black. Mab says it matches my personality, which may be true, but I can lay legitimate claim to the right to wear the ensemble. Thandau took my husband and my son. My husband came back in a wooden box. My son never did. One day I'll make the bastard pay. Until then, my fury will be wasted on those willingly giving aid to the enemy.

Taking on the look wasn't hard. I just let down the walls that I kept up the rest of the time, and the crying came. The experience is actually quite cathartic. It's the only time I allow myself the luxury of tears. There will be time enough for weeping and wailing for the dead once Thandau is among their number.

My naturally white hair was dyed blue. I don't bother with glamours; there are far too many people roaming around with the means to see through the illusion, and that would set me apart from the simple villagers. Poor farm widows can't afford glamours.

The first tavern I went to was called The Club and Foot. It was busy. I made my way in to the barman, making sure to pause and look around warily. Farm widows are nervous types in new places. I pulled out a pair of copper coins, hiding them unskillfully.

"How much for a grand ale?" I asked. The price quoted was much more than my cover identity would have. "What do you have for a copper?"

The barman looked at me with sympathy. As he moved toward me, I could see he was missing his right leg above the knee. He had a wooden one with a locking hinge, skillfully carved, but not magically enhanced. Thandau doesn't take good care of his wounded soldiers. The injured are not much use to him, so he discards them. The man probably had to make the leg himself.

"Stout," he said, then leaned forward and whispered, "But I'll fill the bigger mug in honor of your loss, missus."

A soldier honoring the dead. I could respect that, even from the opposite side. I touched his hand. "My thanks."

He nodded and gave me a sad smile that spoke volumes, followed by the drink.

I meekly stood and raised my glass to make a toast. The room at large ignored my soft words. Remaining in character, I tried a second time with no more luck than the first. The barman took pity on me, or maybe it was just good business. If glasses were drained, they'd have to be refilled. He banged a couple of tankards together and yelled, "Respect for the missus."

The room got quiet, even the cutthroat types. Everyone

had their dead in these wars.

I nodded my gratitude and raised my mug. "To the finest husband a lass ever had! I miss and love you, heart of my heart. Until!" Short for until we meet again.

Glasses raised and more than didn't said, "Until!"

"May those that caused your death die a thousand times."

Glasses raised again, but not as high. It was unclear if I meant those who drafted him or those that did the actual killing. Speaking out against Thandau could be a death sentence. My words were chosen carefully but caused many to be wary. Raising a glass in memory was fine and good, but speaking out against the ruling power was flirting with suicide. A banshee knows all about the many faces of dying. Suicide seems like a cute one from a distance, full of promises and a way out of trouble. Up close, you can see the ugliness, and see that his promises are false. But if you've already allowed him to kiss you, it's far too late to back out of your final date.

Most of Faerie had seen too much death of late, ironic for a world that lets life go on for so long. Death from disease is minimal, but killing each other has always been popular, although never like this. Fey don't reproduce quickly. My husband and I weren't blessed with a child for over a century, though it wasn't for lack of trying. It took a few more years after Jonny to get my twin girls who died alongside their father.

It will take centuries for the population to recover. Goblins and humans have shorter life spans but reproduce so much faster, maybe because they aren't natives. Not that most Fey believe in Earth or humans any more than they believe in us.

I left my toasting at that. A widow daring to speak out directly would be too memorable. One soft stepping around it was common. An angry woman's little jab at an unfair fate would not stand out.

I found a table in the middle of the room and sat. It made me uncomfortable to have people behind me, but the tables in the back corners and along the walls are always the first taken.

Which is when I got lucky.

Most fey don't evolve off into gentry like leprechaun, pixie, or ogre. Many look a lot like humans, except in a greater variety of colors and sizes, with the occasional pointed ear, chin, or nose. Even Banshees don't stand out too much, as long as we keep our mouths shut when it comes time for an endsong. Normally, I have snow-white skin and ivory hair. I make an effort to tan, but it isn't easy. Sometimes I just resort to skin dye.

A fey woman walked in wearing armor, a broadsword, and something nestled beneath her breasts that she never should have had—a silver medallion with a black raven's head. It was the emblem badge of the Daemor. It had been faked in the past. We had been trained to recognize the real thing. This one was the genuine article, which should have been impossible. No Daemor were missing or should even have been near this town. If one were killed, the medallion would have sent a signal so we could locate the body and bring it home. I know every Daemor on sight; I have to, so as not to make a horrible mistake.

This woman wasn't one of us, but the medallion was real. That meant I couldn't just kill her. I had to find the Daemor she took the badge from. If she was alive, I'd rescue her. If she was dead, I'd avenge her. Slowly and painfully.

The question was how. Luck was still with me. The imposter stood up in the center of the barroom and started ranting, not two jumps from me.

"Now is the time to rise up and cast off the shackles of tyranny. I'm looking for a few brave souls to join me in a vital mission to strike at Thandau's very heart." Interesting. She was using our reputation to weed out sympathizers. I doubted her intentions were good. She went on for a while, trying to rile the crowd up. Most tried to ignore her. A few looked like they wanted to tell her to shut up, but a Daemor's reputation was dangerous enough that none dared.

After her impassioned speech, she marched outside, and the room returned to normal. A pair of youths with more guts than hairs on their chins tried to casually sneak out. It was made more obvious by the trying. I waited longer, finished my stout, and returned my mug to the barman.

"My thanks," I said, touching his hand.

"My sympathies," he returned. He seemed a good man. Many others have tried to prey on my supposed vulnerability to have their way with a distraught widow. Nice to see that there were still some decent men left in the world.

I left and scanned the area outside the Club and Foot. The imposter would want to lure would-be traitors to Thandau into her trap. She would not go far. In fact, she was right behind the stables. Four men were hiding nearby, doing a fairly good job of it. Most people wouldn't have noticed them. A Daemor would have to be near passing-out drunk or suffering a still bleeding head wound to not have seen at least three of them.

The youths were strutting and trying to impress the woman. As they told their tales of imagined bravery, neither took their eyes off the cleavage the armor was designed to enhance and prop up. One of the reasons we made it look that way but this woman wore only the skimpy armor. She would be unable to use the glamour as it was tied to its Daemor. The woman was extremely well proportioned—nothing like my fellow Daemor, Terrorbelle, but still impressive—especially next to my meager chest. Perhaps that was part of the reason she was chosen to play the part of the siren leading them to their doom.

When I stepped around the corner, the males jumped and turned on me, ready to growl. They relaxed noticeably when they noticed I was a woman. The impersonator remained cool, but then, she knew she had hidden backup.

"Welcome," said the impersonator.

I played the meek card. "I heard what you said. Thandau took my husband from me. How can I take something from him?"

The pretender smiled. "I will bring all of you to a Daemor stronghold first, where all will be revealed. Let us wait to see if any other brave souls join our campaign."

We spent an hour lurking, but no one else took the bait.

"Let's move out. Keep up," ordered the imposter.

"No problem," said one of the youths, whose name was Han.

"Absolutely," said the other, not wanting to be left out. His name was Wok.

I just nodded and trotted after them into the woods. The quartet hung back, following at a discrete distance.

The pretender was careful to avoid a marked Faerie path. Smart. Wandering on a rambling path can get you lost in time and space or worse, especially if you step off at the wrong spot. In the Daemor, we have a pathmaker, Tralla, who has drilled maps of the majority of the paths into our heads. It's one of our greatest tactical advantages. We can get into and out of places quickly and quietly, while the enemy is hesitant to risk life and sanity by following. I had actually come in on this path.

We trod on for a couple of hours. Occasionally, Han and Wok would attempt some witty banter, but the pretender would shush them, claiming the need for stealth. I got the impression she didn't want to be bothered listening.

We finally arrived at an empty campsite. With a wave of her hand, she lit the pile of wood in the center. Simple survival magiks, but it impressed the youths. Probably neither knew anything beyond the basics like translation spells.

The imposter kept us busy while her companions surrounded us.

"The Daemor is a secret organization." Hardly. We simply hide to survive. The impersonator lifted up her stolen medallion. "This gives me great power." Not true. It's the woman wearing it that has the power. The badge has some serious magic but its true power is in the symbol and what it stands for—the hope of freedom for all of Faerie and the death of tyranny. "What I need all of you to do is swear an oath to me that you will dedicate your lives to fighting Thandau."

"I so swear," said Wok.

"Me, too," quickly chimed in Han, not to be left out.

The imposter looked at me for my oath. "I'd like to know a little bit more about your plan before I swear an oath." Faerie is a magical world. Promises and oaths can become almost tangible things and should not be entered into lightly.

"You are not fully committed to the fight?" asked the pretender, with a tone both scoffing and filled with condescension.

"What fight? All you've done is go on about a fight that you have said nothing about. I wouldn't agree to kill an animal without knowing the how and why, let alone swear an oath to it," I said. As I spoke, the men in the woods were moving in. One wasn't even trying to be quiet. Han and Wok were oblivious.

"She doesn't need to swear the oath," said the noisy one. Han and Wok jumped at the sound. "Just by being here, that's enough to justify conspiracy. For women, we get paid the same either way."

"What's going on here?" said Wok.

"Bounty hunters make a living by taking in traitors," said Noisy.

"That's what we were doing," said Han. "We were going to get the drop on the Daemor and bring her in for the reward."

"Sure, laddie. That'll hold up in the Axe Man's Court," said Noisy.

Axe Courts were set up around the land to dispense death with only a passing nod at justice. The resultant heads kept Thandau's pikes decorated.

"You're no Daemor," I said, feigning indignation and surprise.

The impostor laughed. "You got me. Not that you were smart enough to figure it out before it was too late for you."

"I knew it. That medallion doesn't even look real," I said.

The imposter lifted it up and held it toward me. "Oh, it's real all right. I took it off a Daemor myself."

"She must have died before she'd give it to you," I said.

"She's not dead yet. Axe Man's Court will take care of it tomorrow, though. You'll probably get to watch. The woman was dumb enough to try to come to my rescue. While she was defending me, I smashed her in the back of the head. We got a pretty price for her, and I got to keep this trinket. Enough talking."

I took deep breaths to control my anger. My hair tends to float on its own and my eyes tend to get on the fiery side, which would be counterproductive.

Two of the others wheeled a cart that had been made into a rolling cell. The cart had a balance spell on it, which made it easy for anyone to push it. No beast of burden was necessary. We were all forced into the cell. Although I could have fought back at any point, I let myself be put inside. A Daemor was in danger. That was my first priority. I could kill the bad later.

The ride was bumpy and uncomfortable. I spent the time studying the woman and the men. You can learn much about how well someone can fight by watching them move and walk. This lot could handle themselves, but they were far from experts.

I also wanted to memorize everything about them, as I would have to find them later.

We got to a graycoat outpost jail before sunup. My luck was still holding—it wasn't a Destroyer outpost. The Destroyers were Thandau's elite. They'd be much more thorough searching prisoners, and there was an outside chance I'd be recognized even with my disguise.

We were handed over without incident. The bounty

hunters were given their due. Han and Wok spent the entire time arguing about their innocence. I just wanted into the jail. I ignored as much as I could to keep control of my temper.

The pair of graycoat guards searched the two of them thoroughly. My search consisted less of looking for weapons than feeling out my womanly attributes. Fine by me. I'd suffered worse indignities, and they missed all of my weapons in their groping enthusiasm.

They threw Han and Wok in the first empty cell. I was taken to the back, where they kept the female prisoners. The three incarcerated there weren't treated well. In fact, it seems the graycoat guards thought of them as their own personal brothel, without even granting them the respects of pay or consent.

A pair of guards escorted me, laughing about my upcoming strip search. I ignored them, but they didn't seem to notice. Probably thought I was mute from fear, instead of trying very hard not to kill them.

The last cell held six men. Five held down a woman by her head and limbs while the sixth forced himself on her. She was fighting like a griffin. Judging by the state of undress of the others, he was the third on this shift to do so. I moved so I could see her face. It was Marra, one of the first to be called Daemor. She was a Leanan Sidhe, a member of the gentry. They have often been mistaken for vampyres by mortals, but they have no bloodlust. They can feed off the spirits of others; the energy can be taken or offered. They have been known to inspire poets, musicians, and artists and can feed off the creative energy they give off without harming them. At least in the short term.

They were planning on putting me in the same cell. I waited until the door was opened. An instant later, a pair of needle-thin brain-picks separated the pair of guards' frontal lobes from the rest of their brains. They fell, their spirits fled before their bodies made contact with the floor.

I worked my magic with the picks twice more, on the pair

holding the arm and leg closest to me. I got the pair pinning her other limbs with a poisoned hairpin each.

It hadn't taken three blinks. I could have taken the guards at her head and womanhood in a fourth and fifth blink, but I didn't want to hog all the fun. Marra had suffered much at their hands. She needed a little revenge. It always makes me feel better.

With fewer attackers, she could focus. The rapists didn't stand a chance once she got her natural magiks going. With her hands free, she reached up, pulled the guard holding her head down and locked lips with that attacker. The physical contact triggered an energy drain, and Marra rode the wave as it surged. The drain grew to include the current rapist who hadn't been quick or bright enough to pull out when he saw four of his fellows drop dead. He tried now, but he was too late. Marra wrapped her legs around him, and he had no hope of escape. Minutes later, the pair were withered corpses, and Marra was revitalized, if shaken.

I remained silent until we went down to the guard office and retrieved her armor and weapons. Once she was dressed, she finally looked at me. I could see what it cost her to meet my eyes.

"I was taken down like an amateur," Marra confessed. "They got my badge."

"I know. It's how I found you. We'll get it back but first we have a job to do," I said.

Mara nodded. We both knew standing orders. If an opportunity presents itself to hurt the enemy, do it.

First, we freed the other prisoners. Han and Wok couldn't stop gushing gratitude. The women were hurt badly, both in body and spirit. They would be a long-time healing.

I took point. Our exit was clear and I gave Marra the signal to bring the others out.

We got to the edge of the compound without detection.

We crouched low as a pair of Graycoat sentries moved on their rounds. Han stood and shouted, "Daemor! I've got two Dae—"

Marra slit his throat before he finished his betrayal. I reached and downed both Graycoats with my picks before their swords cleared leather.

Marra and I got on either side of Wok. He fell to his knees. "We were planning to capture the other one for the reward, but you rescued us. I wouldn't have turned on you."

I didn't believe him, but it didn't matter. Someone had to live to tell the tale. We tied him in the upper branches of a tree, and I used a dart coated with paralyzing basilisk venom. He wouldn't be able to move or speak for at least a day. I pointed his head toward the compound.

We ran out back into the woods. There was another ramble path a quarter of an hour's journey away. We got the women on it and brought them to our nearest camp—normally four days away—and handed them over to our medics for healing. One day they might choose to become recruits for Mab's army, or possibly even Daemor once they've proven themselves.

We had a path into a Graycoat compound we didn't know existed a day ago. We had little time before an alarm was raised, if it hadn't been already. I took a squad of Daemor back with me.

We hit the compound running and my luck held. No alarm was raised. We hit the Axe Court and wiped out every last one of the murdering bastards. A lot of Graycoats fell but Daemor aren't murderers—excepting me of course—so we let the wounded flee. Hard to tell the draftees from the volunteers, as they all wear the same uniform. There has to be something that separates us from our enemy. After that, we burned the compound to the ground.

I stopped in the tree where Wok, unable to even close his eyes, had watched the carnage.

"That's what happens when you mess with the Daemor.

Tell everyone you meet. I will come back one day looking for you, and if I do not hear this tale from others, it will not go well for you," I said. I knew he heard and would obey.

My final stroke of luck was when we went to search the town nearby. This one had a tavern called the Rusty Mug. Rust is dangerous poison to fey, so the name let passersby know it wasn't for the weak of heart. A quick recon found the imposter and her crew drinking to their good fortune inside.

I had changed to my Daemor uniform before the battle, including my armor and badge. I even used a small token of power to return my skin and hair to their natural colors.

Daemor guarded all the exits, down to the windows and cellar doors. That's when I let out my endsong. A banshee's wail is known as an omen of death throughout Faerie. It can't be sung unless the final darkness approaches.

As expected, all those assembled within the bar tried to get out. It didn't work, as they all found armed Daemor blocking their paths. No sense in making an example of someone if nobody is there to see. I walked in, Marra at my side. My power was flowing, and I could no longer pass for ungentryfied fey. My hair flew, my eyes bled fire, and my voice summoned the Reaper.

When I turned toward the imposter and her compatriots, they were left alone and deserted by those who had been toasting with them moments before.

"You have ignored the edict that none shall falsely claim to be a Daemor, upon penalty of death. Your lives are now forfeit," I proclaimed.

The five of them jumped up with their swords. As I predicted, they could handle themselves, but Marra was far better with a blade that the lot combined, and claimed the four men in less time than it takes to tell.

By right, the imposter herself fell to me. She held her sword out to defend herself. I screamed. My vocal range is quite good, and my shout was focused on the pretender. Instinctively, she raised her hands up to protect her ears, and as she did, I plucked the sword from her fingers.

Legends abound in Faerie. There is one that claims banshee can claim a life with a single spoken word. I like to encourage that belief.

"Those who do not wish to join the bodies on the floor, shield your ears," I said. Most did as I recommended. The pretender tried to, but I grabbed her right wrist with my right hand. "Except for you." I leaned in to whisper in her ear.

"*Die.*"

That wasn't the word. The problem with using the word is how to keep from hearing it yourself. How do you learn the proper pronunciation without practice? Not to say it can't be done, but it's not easy or safe and there were too many Daemor nearby with excellent hearing.

I pricked her behind the ear with a tiny poisoned needle that dissolves after contact with blood. This particular venom molded the face into a frightened expression that stays as a death masque. It also induces almost instant rigor mortis, which meant she kept her feet until after she was dead. I plucked the Daemor medallion off her chest, then pushed her forehead with a single finger. She fell like a cut tree.

We left without another word. The message was clear, and the bad were dead.

SAD DAYE

A Tale of Daye the Deadly

Another day, another death. Hell of a way to make a living. Heh. It'd be almost funny if it weren't so sad. A few years back if someone had told me I'd end up as the hired blade for Queen Mab's Daemor, I would have told them they were insane. I was a mother and a wife. Now I'm neither thanks to Thandau's graycoats.

I'm still amazed at how deftly I took to killing. True, death is something every banshee is familiar with in ways most fey and gentry will never understand, but to call the Reaper instead of herald his arrival… it channels the hate and anger into something besides tears and sorrow. At first, I hope if I killed enough graycoats the holes in my soul would be filled. Now I know no matter how many I send to the Reaper's embrace that I'll always miss my babies' smiles and my husband's embrace, but the memories of their murderers and their fellow soldiers dying at my hands does actually help me make it through the night.

I do not kill indiscriminately. My job is to kill those who would impede the Daemor and Mab's army and our hopes of an eventual defeat of the tyrant Thandau. And since most of those I send to the Reaper could only be described as evil if you are being charitable, guilt does not stay my hand. More apt descriptions involve words I would never have said in front of my babies. In honor of them, I try not to say those type of things now. Odd I know, an assassin that won't curse, but there you have it.

I walked toward the town of Rough Woods in search of my next gift to the Reaper. Her crime was especially hateful. Daemor cannot compete with Thandau's forces in numbers, materials, or magic. What we did have were our reputations which actually helped keep us safe. People know we follow a code of honor and they know where we stand. Thandau has tried on occasion to turn this strength against us by dressing up women as Daemor and outfitting them with an imitation Daemor badge with a raven's head on a silver circle, then sending them out to do all manner of heinous and evil things to turn the people of Faerie against us. It started to become effective and endanger us, so Mab issued an edict of death against any who dare to impersonate a Daemor. After a dozen or so imposters' heads were hung on strategically placed pikes, the number of impersonators dropped off, but you still get some willing to play the odds. It's my job to find them and made sure they lose that game.

Rough Woods was a Thandau town mainly because he had a large enough army to hold it and strategically it's not vital enough for us to commit our very limited reassures to taking it back. That means the people here have to live under graycoat rule. It's not optimal, but in war, choices have to be made.

There was a Daemor rumored to be operating in the town. One major problem with that – Mab knows where all of our Daemor are and none of them were stationed in Rough Woods. Which of course means the assassin Daye has to ride in and dispatch the imposter.

The woman I used to be is disturbed that I am more troubled that I find myself occasionally speaking in the third person than I am by the prospect of killing a woman.

Sneaking into a Thandau controlled town isn't as hard as one would think. Any town has a need for laborers and most of the laborers don't get more than a cursory examination. Since the poor typically can't afford a glamour, that is the first thing the sentries at town gates look for and why I hardly ever use magic to disguise myself. I find hair dye and body makeup make a much more an effective disguise. However, the key to passing as one of the downtrodden is to lose yourself. And by that, I mean any traces of pride and confidence need to be expelled from how you walk and carry yourself. No making eye contact and no mouthing off regardless of how justified your barbed words might be. It means occasionally having to endure things you would never allow, like a blow or a wandering hand touching flesh that they had no right too. Any hint of defiance is enough to bring you to the attention of even the most dimwitted graycoats.

There were three graycoats on duty at the north gate. Unfortunately, it seemed as though there wasn't as large of an influx of laborers as I had hoped. Only three men and me.

They let the men through after examination and a small bribe from each. Fairly common practice.

It was my turn.

"What have we here?" the ranking graycoat, a gon or sergeant, asked.

"Begging your pardon, sir, I'm just looking for some work for my hands to do. My cousin said that her mistress had need of a seamstress and a cook and I am able to do both of those things."

The graycoat sneered as his eyes wandered up and down my body hungrily. "I see. What do you have to offer us to gain entrance to Rough Woods?"

This was the difficult part. The men had offered handmade items, things that cost nothing but the time and skill of making them. The person I was trying to be would not have much in the way of coins. She would also possibly be unaware of the need for a toll. But I had come prepared.

"I had wanted to prove my skills to my cousin's mistress, so

I baked this pie." I opened the canvas sack of was carrying and pulled out a fruit pie in a wooden bowl. I had, in fact, made it myself. My mothering skills may have been rarely used these days, but they were far from gone.

"It smells delicious," said the youngest looking of the graycoats. He would not have his first beard for a season or two yet and judging by his sleeves, he was a recent recruit without rank.

"Yes, pie is all well and good but you can give that to your cousin's mistress to prove your culinary skills. I have another toll in mind," said the Gon, as he placed his hand upon my buttock and squeezed roughly, with no trace of tenderness.

"Sir, I'm a married woman," I exclaimed, feigning shock.

The Gon laughed, as did the older, fatter graycoat standing next to him. "Then it is probably best that you don't tell him about it, don't you think?"

"But sir, I don't understand," I lied. It must be pretty bad in Rough Woods for the graycoats to be allowing this to go on in the light of day. It pretty hard to keep people in line when they know you are taking advantage of – or outright raping – their mothers, sisters, daughters, and wives. Even the most downtrodden of people start plotting rebellion and worse when faced with that.

"I'm afraid the toll for you will just be a small service," Gon said. "It won't take very much. We can step over here to take care of this business and then you can be on your way."

I figured playing dumb was a better first tactic to take than gutting them in the streets. "But I don't understand …"

"What he is trying to tell you—" the fatass graycoat said. "—is that you are going to service our manly needs." Fatass pumped his pelvis forward a few times to let it be known in no uncertain terms what he had in mind.

"But I can't do that. I'm married," I said.

Gon shrugged. "Then like I said, I guess you had better not

let your husband know about it. The pity for you is that it might just ruin you for other men for the rest of your days, but that is a chance I'm willing to take."

The third graycoat spoke up and I expected him to join the evil fun, but Beardless surprised me.

"Gon, sir, I don't think this is right."

Gon raised his eyebrows. "Excuse me?"

"She's a married lady and she is not willing. There are plenty of women that come through that are more than happy to pay that particular toll," Beardless said.

"Are you suggesting that I take her measly little pie and allow her to come into Rough Woods?"

"Yes, Gon, sir. It would be the soldierly thing to do."

Gon and Fatass looked at each other then back at Beardless. Gon smiled then shoved his fist so far up Beardless' gut that I expected to see his hand come out the other side.

"Then who is going to wax my pole? You? Being a soldier means you take what you are strong enough to get and I do not take insubordination. Consider yourself on report and you are going to be on guard duty for two shifts straight without getting to keep any of the tolls you collect." Beardless was on the ground puking his guts out. It had been an impressive blow. "Do I make myself understood?"

"Yes, Gon."

"Good. Get back on your feet and guard this gate while we take this lady for the time of her life."

I started to back away, but Gon grabbed hold of my arm and yanked me inside of the gate and pulled me towards an alley between what their garrison and what passed for the city wall.

I had already decided I was going to kill them, but it didn't pay to let that be known that ahead of time, so I acted the opposite of how a Daemor would. I screamed and pulled and begged and pleaded for mercy. There was none to be had.

Fatass tried to calm and coax me. "We are really experienced and gifted men. You will truly enjoy it. Trust me."

I trusted Fatass about as far as I could throw his decapitated head. I responded by dropping to the floor kicking and screaming. The soldiers laughed. Fatass grabbed me under the legs and Gon grabbed me under the arms and around the chest, apparently mistaking my breasts for handles. The two of them carried me into the alley and ended my unpleasant journey with a toss into a wall. Fortunately, I had anticipated their action and moved so the blow was spread out throughout my body. Gon had already undone his sword belt and had his pants dropped down to his ankles.

"You best get your dress up and off, Missus. Things will go better for you if I am not forced to beat you." I decided now would be an excellent time to take them out, maybe see just how far I could throw Fatass's decapitated head. I was again surprised. Apparently, I was not the only one planning to stop the graycoats.

"Step away from that woman," came a voice from atop the city wall. The three of us looked up to see a woman in form-fitting armor that exposed as much skin as it protected. On this woman's chest was a circle of silver with a raven's head on it. These idiots had helped me find the fake Daemor.

"It's her! Sound the alarm," Gon said to Fatass, but before the big man could move the woman leapt off the wall, her boot connecting with his face making the back of his head strike the garrison wall. Fatass closed his eyes and sank to the pavement.

The woman already had her sword drawn and Gon's was on the ground next to his fallen pants.

"I thought you graycoats knew that the people in this town were under my protection. The protection of a Daemor."

"Shut up, whore," Gon said, spitting on the woman's face. She brought her boot up into his groin, with him hitting the ground harder and faster than when he struck Beardless.

Although it was no doubt satisfying to hit the graycoat in that most sensitive of male places, it was an amateur move because it knocked him to the ground where he was able to reach out for his weapon. He pulled the sword from the sheath and thrust it towards the woman's heart. With a deft movement of her wrist she knocked the blade away and made a thrust of her own directly into Gon's throat. The sword exited out through his spine, causing his body to twitch and then lie still. She removed the blade and there were a few gurgles as Gon's own blood started to drown him. Within moments he was dead, the loss of blood getting him before the suffocation.

The false Daemor offered me her hand. I took it. I should have ended her right then and there, only something seemed odd. All the other imitation Daemor had been working with the graycoats to make us look bad. This one seemed to have her own agenda and I wanted to find out exactly what that was and if there were any more like her.

"Are you okay?"

Making sure to maintain my character I answered, "I am, thanks to you. How can I show my appreciation?"

The woman smiled.

"No need for thanks. A Daemor's job is to help the helpless. Do you have a place to stay in the city? Or should I help you get outside of the wall before this comes down on you?" she said.

"I had the possibility of a job, otherwise I really have nowhere else to go. The graycoats conscripted all the men in my town and took the woman for worse. I managed to sneak away and I have been looking for a way to support myself since," I lied.

"An all too familiar fate these days, it is sad to say. Okay, I have a place for you to get your bearings straight. They will take care of you, feed you, and see about finding you some gainful employment." The false Daemor reached into a waist pouch and pulled out a hooded cloak and quickly put it on. She stood in such a way that the too large robe made her look masculine. She offered me her arm. It was a way for men to offer a woman their protection from others. I took it and we walked quickly out back past the garrison and down another alleyway to merge onto the main street.

"What is your name?" she asked.

"Janna," I lied. Daye is not an overly common name but it is well known as the name of the Daemor assassin and I didn't want to give her any reason to disappear on me. "What is yours?"

"Mace," she said and led me on a complicated path. We walked weaving back and forth through alleys and side streets with Mace constantly looking behind, above and around us to make sure we were not being followed. I had to admit she was very competent. As we turned to go in an alleyway I noticed her go out of her way to step on a stone and seem to stumble and hit another stone on a wall. She then changed her gait to step on several more stones. As we turned the corner the ground literally opened up.

"Stay close to me, otherwise you will be caught when it closes," Mace said, grabbing hold of my hand and leading me downstairs that had appeared below the sprung trap door. Our heads had barely cleared the ground, which became the ceiling once the opening closed. The place was pitch black. I fell out of character, readying for an attack.

Instead, Mace led me through the darkness. I heard her pushing a combination of stones on the floor again. A door opened and light filled the corridor.

"It was designed so that the two doors can't be opened at the same time. This way if it was ever used at night, the light couldn't betray where we were going to anyone that was watching from above," Mace said.

"Amazing." I was suitably impressed. That only increased as I looked around. The underground chamber was housing men, women, and children. Nearly fifty by my count.

"Who are all these people?"

Before I could get my answer, a young girl ran over, her arms flung wide, directly at Mace. The imitation Daemor scooped up the girl in a hug.

"Mace, you're back! Was there any trouble out there?" the girl said.

Mace laughed. "Nothing I couldn't handle."

"You mean nothing a Daemor couldn't handle," the girl said. "I want to be a Daemor just like you when I grow up."

"A very worthy aspiration, but it is a lot of hard work and training. Until then you have to listen to everything your mother tells you and not give her a hard time," Mace said.

"I know. Who is the lady?"

"This is Janna. Some mean graycoats were trying to hurt her," Mace said.

"But you saved her, didn't you? Just like you saved the rest of us," the girl said.

Now I was truly confused. Why would Thandau's imitation Daemor be helping his victims?

"So Mace helped all of you?"

"Oh yes. She helps others too but many of them had places of their own. All of us didn't have anywhere else to go. We couldn't go home after they killed my father," the girl said. "The soldiers tried to take mommy and me away, but Mace stopped the slave transport and rescued all of us."

"You stopped an entire slave caravan by yourself?" I said incredulously. That was a feat worthy of a true Daemor.

Mace smiled modestly and shrugged. "It was weeks in the planning and I had to lay out many traps. But yes, I did."

"Before Mace got here everyone was afraid of the graycoats. The Daemor didn't bother much with us because we were kind of in the middle of nowhere. That all changed when Mace got here because now the graycoats are afraid of her."

"I wouldn't say they were afraid of me. I'd say I'm more of a huge pain in their bottoms. Now Janna, can we get you something to eat?"

I hesitated a minute sizing up Mace. She was behaving like a real Daemor would. In fact, by housing these people, she was going above and beyond what most Daemor had to do. Mab ran havens for refugees, so usually all a Daemor had to do was drop off anyone in need of hiding or a home and then head back out to the field. It seemed Mace was truly a freedom fighter, dedicated to the same cause as Mab's forces. It was just unfortunate that she chose to claim to be a Daemor. There were no exceptions in Mab's edict allowing for mercy just because the impersonator meant well. For the first time in a very long time, I felt sorry for one of my targets.

"Thank you, but I'm not very hungry right now," I said truthfully. I felt sick to my stomach over the thought of losing her to the Reaper.

"Nonsense, you have to keep up your strength," said Mace.

"I have a pie, although I'm happy to share." I handed it to the girl.

"Excellent. We shall have dessert tonight, but what good is a snack without a meal? Have some soup and maybe some bread. Janna bring her some."

The little girl did and I ate it. It wasn't bad, no worse than the army food I was used to. My slender piece of my pie was much better. Everyone who wanted some was given a small slice. It was good enough that many of the eaters liked me immediately. Good food has that effect. Maybe even why the false Daemor fed these people.

I made my way around the underground hideaway and talked with the others. Mace seemed to be genuinely helping these people. One of them was even her cousin. Apparently, her parents were well off and were able to pay bribes to the graycoats to leave their family alone, but Mace couldn't look the other way when helpless people were being hurt. She dyed and cut her hair as a disguise so her family didn't get any retribution for her actions. According to her cousin, she disappeared for a couple months and came back as a Daemor. I kept silent on the truth that it took much longer for a woman to become one of Mab's elite forces.

After what was likely nightfall, Mace left to go out again. I snuck out after her, following her like a shadow. Again, no magic, just stealth training. She didn't notice me as I followed her onto the streets.

She took to the rooftops, which made sense. Most people tend not to look up and the buildings in Rough Woods were close enough to allow people to leap from one to the other. It was a way to patrol and minimize the chance of being caught. As the night went on, I watched her stop thieves who were attacking a single man, then steal food many times over from the richer neighborhoods only to drop it at the poorer ones.

My reservations about introducing her to the Reaper were increasing. If nothing else, we should recruit her for the army and she could make her way up to Daemor.

I was trying to think up a way to convince Mab to recruit rather than kill when I heard a woman scream. I ran back the way I came along the rooftops until I came upon an alley where Fatass from earlier had cornered a girl all of twelve, bolstered by a half-dozen other soldiers looking for an especially evil way to spend their downtime. Fatass already had his pants down around his ankles and was pointing a sword in the girl child's direction. The other soldiers were lining up behind him in wait for their own turns. I leapt down, feet hitting against the far wall and pushed off again towards the wall of the building I started on, landing on the ground between Fatass and the girl.

"You have one chance to live. Walk away now," I said.

Fatass laughed in my face. "I am not afraid of you, woman. I have no reason to be."

"You should. I'm a Daemor."

That stopped Fatass from laughing, but he didn't look like he believed me. I was still in character both in posture and manner. It was enough for his companions to draw their swords and one of them to pull a bow.

Now there are plenty of stories about Daemor – how we're are stronger than giants and faster than flying arrows but most of them we allow to be spread to give us a psychological advantage over our enemies in battle. Yes, an arrow can be caught by most Daemor – we are trained to do it– but at this close a range there isn't time to prepare properly so I wasn't exactly confident at my odds.

"Shoot her just in case she's speaking the truth," Fatass ordered.

The bowman let the shaft loose. I reached out in hopes of catching it, but it never reached me. Instead, Mace jumped from the rooftop straight down, taking the arrow meant for me right in her chest.

"Mace," I said. I wanted to ask if she was okay, but I knew she wasn't. They had gotten her heart. The native magic of Faerie extends life, but it has its limits. She had moments.

I cradled her in my arms and she grabbed my chest. "I have a confession …" she said. As she reached for my shawl, her hand touched a round disc underneath it. Mace pulled the cloth off and saw my Daemor badge. Her eyes went wide in amazement and awe.

"No need for confessions. You are one of us," I said. Loud enough for both her and the graycoats to hear.

"I knew you would come. Did you mean that I really was one of you?"

"In almost every way that counts," I whispered.

"Somebody has to take care of Rough Woods," she whispered.

"Rough Woods will be taken care of. I promise."

"The word of a Daemor, so I know it's true," she said with a smile. I sang my song of death and the light went out of her eyes. I reached in her scabbard and drew her sword, then gently laid her body on the ground before I stood up to face the murdering, raping bastards that killed her. Fatass took a step back, now able to see my Daemor badge.

"Maybe we will give you a chance, Daemor. There are seven of us and one of you. Walk away and we will let this go," Fatass said.

"You don't understand. You just killed a Daemor."

Yes, I was supposed to kill her and in a way I guess I did. Mace put herself in harm's way to save my life. I wasn't so far gone that the irony and guilt didn't eat me up inside, which only fueled my anger. I pushed it down inside. Anger in battle makes a warrior sloppy.

Mace had behaved with the honor of a Daemor. Everyone believed Mace to be a Daemor. I came here to enforce one of Mab edicts and I was damn well going to do it. I was just choosing a different one.

"Anyone that harms a Daemor pays the ultimate price."

"We still outnumber you," Fatass said.

"Think so? Then perhaps I should tell you my name. I am Daye." I saw the color drain out of Fatass's face and I activated the glamour so I appeared to be wearing skimpy armor, but it just covered my clothes. "It's nice to see my reputation precedes me."

"Shoot her again," he ordered.

The bowman tried, but now I wasn't barehanded. With the sword I swatted the arrow aside, making sure it didn't hit the girl who was the greatcoat's original target. I lunged forward and my blade was through his throat and out the back of his neck before he could blink. Without breaking stride, I grabbed two arrows from the archer's quiver and rammed them through the eyes of two more of the graycoats. I used my bare hands to snap the neck of a fourth and a pair of poison-tipped hairpins on the fifth and the sixth. That just left Fatass. I turned toward him and he started to run away. I was on him before he got out of the alley. Fatass wasn't getting off that easy – his introduction to the Reaper was going to be something extra special.

"Go on get out of here and get home," I said to the girl. "Tell everyone to stay indoors. The graycoats killed a Daemor. By morning, there will not be a single graycoat left alive in Rough Woods." The girl nodded and ran off. It was good because I didn't want to scar her by having her watch what I was about to do to Fatass. I had barely begun before he started screaming and as much as I hate to admit it, it was music to my ears.

And it turns out that I got quite some distance when I tossed his head.

I was good, but to take out an entire garrison of soldiers – that took more than one Daemor. I needed reinforcements. Of course, that didn't mean I couldn't soften things up a bit. I made a few preparations to the garrison for my return and left Rough Woods by going over the wall. Of course, to do so I had to send two guards to the arms of the Boneman. That just meant they were going to get a head start on their fellow graycoats.

Daemor have an asset that Thandau doesn't and it is one of the few things that's allowed us to stay alive and fight Thandau's superior numbers and resources. Her name is Tralla and she is a pathmaker. There are lots of mages that are pathfinders, but Tralla can make and change fairy paths. On a path, time and space warp so you can make journeys that would take weeks or months on foot in a matter of seconds. Of course, go down one the wrong way and come back at a slightly different angle and everyone you ever knew could be ancient.

As part of Daemor training we have to memorize the paths so we know how to get from one part of Fairy to another. I ran for almost an hour to get to the nearest path but it took me less than four minutes on the paths to get to Mab's castle. It was the middle of the night when I got there, but Mab was woken up to hear my report. I waited for her in the throne room. It didn't take her long to arrive dressed in full armor. You would never know that moments before she had been asleep.

"Any particular reason this couldn't wait until morning?" said Mab. "I assume the imposter is dead?"

"Yes, but therein lies our problem. It seems that the imposter was not working to discredit us. In fact, if anything she was bolstering our reputation."

Mab turned her head and narrowed her eyes. "Explain."

I did, telling how Mace had worked to protect the innocent, feed the hungry, and house the homeless. "And she was killed by the soldiers because they thought she was a Daemor."

"I see." Mab became silent. I could see the muscles in her jaw tighten. "So you feel since people thought she was a Daemor, that we should avenge her?"

I nodded. "I do, my queen."

"We could simply disavow her."

"Mab, she died saving me and a child. She embodied everything the Daemor stand for. I owe her a debt that I can never repay directly to her. I respectfully request that she posthumously be declared a Daemor for service above and beyond. Therefore, she would be deserving of vengeance upon those who killed her."

"Strategically speaking, there is nothing to be gained by taking the town."

"While that may be true, from a perception standpoint there is much to be achieved. People will see that you don't hurt a Daemor and come away from it unscathed. They will be shown that the Daemor care enough to free a town that is not strategically important. It will help us win the hearts and the minds of some. And maybe it will give others hope against the tyrant and that might even lead to new recruits for our army."

"Excellent points all, but it is not worth the deployment of manpower. I will have to turn down your request."

"Then I tell you that I will have to resign my position," I said.

Mab's head snapped as she stared at me. "You will no longer be a Daemor?"

"No, once a Daemor always a Daemor. However, I will not be able to serve as your assassin. You know it is a job that I find distasteful, but necessary. However, my debt to Mace will force me to take her place in Rough Woods. As a Daemor, of course. I will not have the time to function as your blade."

"I could order you to remain," said Mab.

"Yes, you could, but that would be in direct contradiction to our agreement. When I became your assassin, you told me I could quit anytime and name my new position. I am evoking that part of our agreement. Should you order me to do otherwise, I will of course obey, but we both know you will not break your word."

Mab took a deep breath in. "Very well, here is my compromise. You can accept it or not. You may take any Daemor who are in residence with you so long as they are willing to volunteer for this mission. Should you get enough takers to join you in this… foolishness, I will grant your request that Mace be made an *honorary* Daemor."

"Thank you, Mab." She nodded again and my audience was over. I left quickly and headed to the dormitory tower. I woke several Daemor from their slumber and got my volunteers. Kande, a human from Earth who joined our cause and fights with sword and one of the few guns that actually works in Faerie. Terrorbelle, half ogre, half pixie, all warrior. Bristlebrite, a pixie with the heart of a giant. Saraid the roane, a shape-changing seal woman who, like many of us, lost much to Thandau including one of her human eyes. Elon, an intelligent horse who worked her way up from a mount to a full-fledged warrior. And last, but certainly not least, the mighty Smaze, who was the offspring of a fire and a water dragon. Seven women against two hundred soldiers. My head knows that the odds are in the soldiers' favor, but my heart knows that they don't stand a chance.

Once we left the path, it took us a third of an hour to return to Rough Woods. Terrorbelle and Bristlebrite flew under their own power while Smaze carried Saraid and me. Kande rode on Elon. The pair had been friends since they accompanied Mab on her return from a brief exile on Earth, back before the mare gained intelligence.

A full-frontal assault would be suicide if the graycoats had found the bodies and heard what I had told the girl about us coming back.

We needed cover. Because of her parentage, Smaze's body was constantly at war with itself. While she could neither breathe fire nor pure water, she was able to put out various mixtures of the two. The dragon opened her mouth and exhaled a heavy fog that covered the main gate and the surrounding town. Brsitlebrite went in first to recon the garrison.

Before I left, I had weakened the support beams of the soldiers' barracks. The pixie emerged from a window to hover above the fog and gave the all clear sign. Terrorbelle flew over the wall, as did Smaze who carried Elon in her talons and Kande on her back. Each took a separate wall, except for Kande who took a rope I had prepared and tied it to the mare. The wall closest to the graycoats on sentry duty was left empty so as not to attract undue attention too early. Bristlebrite flew from wall to wall to make sure everyone was set and gave the signal by changing the sound of her wings buzzing. The dragon, the horse, and Terrorbelle pulled, then pulled again. Smaze's wall was the first to fall. Next went Terrorbelle's and finally Elon's, until the roof collapsed, crushing the sleeping graycoats within.

Next Saraid and I slipped over the wall of the main gate, hoping the distraction of the falling building would cover our entry. It did. I dispatched the graycoat nearest to me, Saraid did the same. She got to the third before I did, her blade pulled back for the killing stroke.

The last graycoat was Beardless.

"Stop!" I whispered and Saraid stopped her blade a finger's width from Beardless' throat. "He tried to stop the others. He'll be our messenger." We needed one alive to tell the tale.

I took some rope and tied Beardless, tearing his own sleeve to gag him. "You live only because you tried to do the right thing. Try to escape or sound an alarm and you will suffer the same fate as your fellows. Clear?"

Beardless nodded and Saraid cocked him on the back of the head with the hilt of her sword. We weren't about to simply trust the boy, should he happen to wake up before we were done he will hopefully think better of doing something foolish. We blindfolded him as the less he could relay to the graycoats, the better.

What happened next was not pretty. According to Bristlebrite's estimation, almost one hundred and fifty enemy soldiers had been inside the garrison when we brought it tumbling down. Smaze covered the rubble with scalding steam she spat out, boiling any flesh inside, making sure the Reaper claimed any of those who might have survived beneath the fallen mortar and timbers.

We hit the three other gates next. Terrorbelle and Bristlebrite rained death from the skies at the east and west gates respectively, each taking out a trio of sentries. Kande and Elon took out the three at the south gate. Saraid and I each went down the main street, looking for graycoats while Smaze watched from the air, able to see through her fog better than the rest of us. The roane and I came up empty until we hit the first tavern we found. Everyone but Smaze joined us as we entered. The dragon kept watch outside. Inside we found twenty drunken graycoats.

"We Daemor claim vengeance for our fallen sister," I

announced after I had already started killing. Three of Thandau's soldiers hit the wooden floor before I finished the sentence.

Bristlebrite's armor was a weapon, her helmet and gauntlets functioned as blades. The pixie dove down, slicing one soldier's jugular with an arm and literally going in one side and out the other of a second soldier's throat using her helmet. Elon bucked, her hooves crushing rib cages. Kande shot again and again, each time hitting a graycoat. Saraid's blades seemed to swim through the air with a deadly grace, finding target after target. Terrorbelle grabbed two soldiers by their heads and smashed their skulls together, reducing them to a bony mush.

I simply sang, reducing most of the remaining soldiers to trembling cowards who quickly tried to run away. The song of the banshee is not for the weak hearted.

Not a one made it past me.

It was much the same in the next several bars and a whorehouse. By dawn's first light, Beardless was the only remaining graycoat left alive in Rough Woods. And although we received our share of wounds, no Daemor fell.

I dragged the boy soldier out the city gate he had guarded, untying his legs and removing his gag, but leaving his hands tied behind his back and his blindfold on.

I shoved him to his knees so he faced the city wall before removing his blindfold. Beardless opened his eyes, looked up at me and screamed.

He had good reason to. I allowed some of my banshee aspect to show through. When the Reaper is coming to call and for a while after, banshee are able to take on some of Death's many aspects. Right now, my face looked more skull than flesh. Even more terrifying than my visage was the dozens of his fellow graycoats looking down upon him, their lifeless heads placed upon pikes atop the wall.

Beardless crawled away from me, his legs pushing so hard that he slid on his back in the dirt.

"Tell your masters this is the price of hurting a Daemor. This city is ours now. Any graycoats who dare return will suffer the same fate."

Beardless rolled over and managed to get to his feet, running away as fast as his legs could carry him, still screaming all the while.

I stood and watched until he was out of sight. Only then did my fellow Daemor allow themselves to come out of hiding. Again, the less the greatcoats knew about who had taken the city, the better it would go for us. We knew they would return to attack in force. We had time to fortify Rough Woods and train the citizens to defend themselves against the coming attack. In our favor now was Rough Woods was of no more strategic value to Thandau than it was to us. If a full attack failed, the tyrant might leave it alone for a time.

And with luck, before he was inclined to try again, we'll have his head upon a pike. Unlikely, but the thought of it warms the cold parts of my heart and gives me a reason to go on.

Virgin Territory

A Tale of the Daemor Kande and Elon

About the time I first left Earth, a movie was sporting the tagline "you'll believe a man can fly". The bozos who attacked me seemed bound and determined to prove that line true. Get enough liquor in local toughs and they think they're warriors. It gives them the idea and the courage to try and attack a Daemor. They figure the legends about we female warriors couldn't possibly be true. A second after they attack me, they become airborne. When they landed, they kicked up clouds of sawdust. I'm not without pity. They're dumb kids like I was back in Brooklyn, so I work hard not to hurt them too much, just enough to make them limp a few days and learn their lesson.

My lesson would be to remember to put my mug down before I start roughhousing. I tend to spend too much effort protecting the rather pitiful ale that passes for booze in these parts.

The sad part is I wasn't alone. My companion is also a Daemor, but so far she hadn't lifted a hoof to help me. She's been watching with amusement and whinnying with laughter.

"I'm glad you think this is so funny, Elon," I said, spinning so my hand sent a charging ruffian headfirst into the nearest wall.

The dun-colored mare nodded her head and neighed. Elon's been in Faerie long enough that exposure to magic has exponentially increased her intelligence and language skills, but she chooses not to lower herself to actually speak human if it can be avoided. It was rarely an issue since *her human* was bright enough to understand horse. I hate it when she calls me that.

Of course, she has to criticize me while I'm working. No thought of waiting until I was done so as not to distract me. Sure, I'm very good, but even the good make mistakes and sometimes even the bad get lucky.

Her latest commentary was on my fashion sense or in her opinion, lack thereof.

"I look fine." Elon whinnied. "And I'm not going to stop wearing my uniform." A glamour actually hid my armor.

One of my attackers, an unfortunate looking pugish man whose appearance literally reeked of ogre ancestry, was closing in on me barehanded. Of course, either of his fists was easily larger than my head. I found some comfort in the look in his eyes. He had no interest in robbery or rape, just a drunken test of his mettle. Barehanded earned him brownie points too, not to mention saving him some nasty flesh wounds. The sword and gun I wore on my belt weren't for show. Neither were the throwing daggers on my legs or my wrist stabbers, metal bands with spring-loaded blades, nor the various other weapons I carried on my person. If it was that kind of fight, I'd already be done and downing my drink to drown the nausea that killing still gives me, even after all these years. These yahoos were looking for a challenge, not suicide.

"You could remove the uniform if you like. It really doesn't cover much of your beautiful ebony skin." Great, even on a world where people have green and pink skin, I still get hassled for being black. "I'd be willing to wait until you were done," the pugish man said, punctuating his words with a leer.

I suppose he wasn't wrong about my uniform in terms of parts covered. The glamour made it look like I wore blue jeans on my lower body. My upper body armor would blend in just fine at Rockaway Beach as a metal bikini. The only thing that would set it apart was the silver and black raven emblem nestled at the lowest midpoint of my cleavage. That emblem makes all the difference to me and I liked to share my differences with others, in this case, Pugface.

I wrapped my fingers around his throat before he knew what was happening. Pugface was several times stronger than me but had the barest fraction of my experience. I knew where the pressure points in his throat were and how to use them to kill him, knock him unconscious, or just cause him pain. I picked choice three and increased the pressure when he tried to back away. Pain tends to make people behave.

That's when I got Brooklyn on his ass.

"You got a problem with this uniform, Pug? Friends of mine died in this uniform."

Some wiseass said, "I hope you cleaned it before you put it on."

He shut up real fast when my dagger plunked into the wall next to his right cheek, close enough to draw blood.

"You want to take this to the next level, punk? The Daemor wore this uniform when they fought to free every one of you from Thandau. People I loved gave all for this uniform. Under no circumstances will I let anyone diss this uniform." My entire tirade was growled through gritted teeth. It wasn't a show – it was my temper and I needed to get it under control. Mab always taught us anger equals dead in battle. I wasn't angry enough to die.

Pugface tired even harder to get away, but I switched my grip to choice two. He was started to turn purple and was undoubtedly seeing stars. His eyes widened until his pupils looked black. Confused and trapped, he decided to try for small talk. "Diss?"

"Earth slang for disrespect."

"Earth?"

"Earth."

Some idiot who thought he was a ninja was sneaking up behind me. Without looking, I slammed my fist up sharply into the fey's nose. The ninja wannabe fell over unconscious.

"You fellows want to take back what you said or do we take this party to a whole 'nother level?"

"I take it back! I am so sorry. Please forgive me," begged Pugface. There were tears in his eyes and liquid dripping from his nose as he groveled. The loudmouth next to my blade in the wall was spouting similar feelings.

I headbutted Pugface and he gave a little yelp of pain as he passed into unconsciousness. "Let me think about it. "

I looked over at loudmouth and he pretended to faint. I walked over to retrieve my dagger and kicked him only once. To his credit, he contained his yell and didn't ruin his unconscious act.

"Anybody else wanna make a comment?"

Three toughs remained standing. Two of them looked at me then at the men on the floor, and finally at each other before they raced out the door. The third picked up a chair and threw it at me. I leaned back so that it missed me, but it struck a glancing blow on my tankard. I spilled some of my drink.

"Now you've got me pissed," I yelled, mainly because it wasn't good enough to pay for the first time, let alone a second. Since he started the throwing, I figured I'd finish it. I flung the metal tankard across the room and it made hard and fast contact with the forehead of the chair thrower. Judging by how his pupils dilated, the hit caused his world to become very bright for a brief moment, which was long enough for me to rush across the barroom. I hit him in the stomach, then slapped him across his face. I slapped him again, hard enough to make him topple sideways.

I grabbed his shirt and pulled him back to his feet, only to slap him down again. I repeated the process half a dozen times.

This guy wasn't all that tough and in the morning the slaps would hurt less than the beating I gave his friend loudmouth.

Finally, Chairthrower held up a hand and mumbled, "Wait!"

I obliged.

"How about I buy you another drink? And one for your horse, too?"

I tilted my head to the side as if contemplating the offer. I turned to the *fjord* and my faithful equine companion whinnied, then nodded.

I wrapped my arm around the man's neck so the back of his head rested in the crock of my elbow. Thinking a blow was coming, chair thrower winced, but instead I gave him a nuggie.

"Buy us drinks? Why didn't you just say so? We could've avoided all this nonsense," I said, thumping him on his back, only slightly harder than I needed to. Chairthrower had to brace himself to keep from being knocked to the ground.

"Bartender, set up rounds for my horse and for me, courtesy of my new friend..."

"Joer."

"...Joer. I hope you're not strapped for cash, 'cause we're a couple of party girls." And frankly, cash was always tight with us.

"You drink that much?" asked Joer.

"Sometimes but Elon can drink an ogre under the table. Tonight should prove to be impressive as she is trying to forget a broken heart. Her latest love galloped off without even saying goodbye."

The bartender had filled a bucket with beer and placed it on the bar top. Elon trotted over, whinnied, shook her head, then hit her right front hoof on the bar twice. The bartender shrugged, filled another bucket and set it by the first. The fjord drank some from each bucket, then grabbed both handles in her mouth and took the drinks back to our table. Once they were set down, Elon turned back and whinnied at Joer.

"She says thanks," I translated.

"You're welcome, horse." The mare winked at Joer.

"I think she likes you. A word of advice—when she drinks too much Elon doesn't care much about species. For your own protection, I wouldn't get too close." I motioned to have my drink freshened.

Joer's pupils got wide. "You're kidding."

"Nope."

Joer looked nervous. "I'll remember your advice."

"Good. Thanks for the cocktails," I said, lifting the refilled tankard from the bar. "I hope you're not expecting me to put out just because you bought me a drink."

"Put out what?"

Again, I translated. "Try to bed me."

Joer expression was one of pure panic. "Um, I would never dream of..."

"Relax Joer, I'm playing you. But never stop dreaming of something better. That's something I learned as a girl when I dreamed of visiting magical lands. Pity it took a war to make it come true. I'm talking too much." I tended to do that in the afterglow of a won fight or sex. "Next time, just be more careful who you start a fight with." I turned my back with a wink and a wiggle in my walk that in my younger days would have made the boys blather about getting a burger with that shake. I agree using my sex appeal to tease someone is immature, but hey, I do basically walk around in a chainmail bikini with tight jeans. I'd be lying if I admitted the effect it had on the opposite sex had nothing to do with it, but I'd never let a man give me grief about it.

Elon on the other hoof was another matter. She let me have it when I got back to the table.

"I am not a tease but you're a nag, in every sense of the word." The horse rolled her eyes back. "Who are you to talk?

We both know why he left you."

Elon tried an expression of innocence and for a horse, succeeded remarkably well.

"You're a shameless hussy. You cheated on the unicorn with a plow horse." Elon did some suggestive neighing and wiggled her eyebrows. "Of course, he was hung like a horse. You know why? Because he's a horse."

Elon made a dismissive raspberry-like sound by blowing through her lips.

"Ahem," said a short fey, who was standing meekly at the far end of our table. We had heard him approach. It had been almost amusing the care he took to make quite a bit of noise in an effort to make it clear he was not sneaking up on us. We had been ignoring him until he said something and it looked like that moment had arrived.

The fey was tall, broad and with chiseled arms. Handsome if you like that sort of thing. He was dressed like a farmer, with thick, dark, and durable clothes. Not that that meant anything in the scheme of things. It could be a disguise or he had a fondness for those type of clothes. His eyes kept darting nervously around the room, which gave me the impression he wasn't a local.

"Can we help you?" I asked.

The man sighed like he had been holding his breath for some time. "Oh, I certainly hope so. My name is Aiden. I've been searching long and far for someone like you."

Despite the phrasing, I didn't think it was a pick-up line. "And you didn't even ask me my sign."

"I don't understand."

"Nobody around here ever does." A stranger in a strange land and all that. "Okay, you've found me. Now what? Is it your turn to hide and mine to try and find you?"

The man's tongue seemed tied, maybe even chained. Other parts of him seemed to move more freely, most notably the front pocket of his trousers. It was vibrating and seemed to be glowing. Not something a lady ever likes to see. Well, almost never anyway.

I slid my hand down to my holster, slipped off the leather strap and slid out my magnum

"So, is that a flashlight in your pocket or are you just happy to see me?" My gun was now trained on the fey's belly, still out of sight beneath the table.

"What?" The man again appeared confused. "I'm not sure what a flashlight is, but what is in my pocket makes me very happy to see you indeed."

Aiden reached into his pocket, but before he could extract anything, my dagger was again in my other hand in a throwing posture. The gun was infinitely more effective, but not everyone in Faerie was familiar with firearms, since very few work after a month or so. The meaning of the dagger was unmistakable, especially that it was made out of steel. Most of we humans fall short of the natives in mystic abilities, but all of us could handle iron.

"No sudden moves there, Aiden."

Aiden threw his arms up in the air. That section of the bar quickly cleared out. "Please, it's not a weapon. It's a *delve*, a seeker gem. Reach into my pocket and pull it out yourself."

"Like I haven't heard that one before. You take it out, nice and slow. Anything funny happens and you're dead, understand?"

"I assure you, there is nothing funny about this. It's a matter of life and death, many times over."

"Then get on with it."

With exaggerated slowness and care, Aiden removed the delve from his pocket and its white glow intensified.

"See? It has chosen you," said Aiden, holding the bright stone out to me. "Please, take it."

I laid the dagger on my lap and reached out. As my hand made contact, the light intensified until it was practically blinding. Putting the gem on the table I reached into the pack on Elon's back with my free hand and removed a pair of dark sunglasses from back home.

"A dragon threatens my home and I was sent out to find one who could save us."

"So, I'm the chosen one?" I asked.

"Yes, exactly," said Aiden excitedly.

Elon lifted her head back and her Mohawk-like mane shook with laughter.

"Shut up! Is it so hard to believe that I might be a chosen one?" I'd been doing this warrior woman thing for a long time, but I'd never been a chosen. I'd helped out a few, but it was an always a bridesmaid, never a bride kind of thing. I'd never even realized I cared until this point.

Elon tilted her head to one side and looked up in contemplation, before nodding her head several times. I ignored her.

"Aiden, please sit and tell me the whole story. My name is Kande and this lazy pile of walking dog food is Elon."

"A true pleasure. My story is a frightful one. Hardscrabble is a very small town, without much by way of goods or people. Mostly, we are farmers. Very few outsiders take notice of us since the end of the war. A few weeks ago, that changed. Somehow we attracted the attention of a dragon."

"A dragon? What kind?" Dragons are elemental creatures, although I've met some interesting crossbreeds.

"A fire dragon. The beast demanded tribute or promised to destroy us."

I shrugged. "Dragons are people like the rest of us. Some are good and others aren't." Dragons demanding tribute isn't new, I just hadn't heard of it happening lately. "What did she want? Gold, jewels, livestock?"

"Far more than that. _He_ demanded a virgin."

"That doesn't make sense. Why would a dragon want a

virgin?" I asked. Elon raised her eyebrows suggestively as she wiggled her horse hips. "That's not physically possible, Elon. The physics alone boggles the mind."

"There are legends about it," Aiden said.

"I've dealt with dragons before, as both allies and adversaries. Not one of them would care about a person's sexual status, even the evil ones looking for a sentient meal. They'd be more likely to ask for the plumpest."

"I can't speak for other dragons, I only know what I heard this one ask for. He made his demands in front of most of the town. Our elders sent some of us out to find those who can aid the town and I found you. Are you willing to help us? I know it is a great sacrifice we are asking of you..."

"I don't know about that. I'll try to negotiate with it first. Maybe it'll take a pig or something instead. If not, Elon and I will just have to persuade it to go elsewhere," I said. Dragons were tough and intelligent but not invincible. With some planning and a few tricks, we'd have a halfway decent chance of winning. The fjord nodded and grunted her agreement. It was followed by a loud belch and a hoof covering an embarrassed expression. Elon knew the meaning of the word couth, she just thought it applied to others instead of her. "You'll have to pardon her. She was raised in a barn."

Elon put her two cents in. "Don't you go trashing the projects." More equine commentary. "Yes, I do think it was a better place to be brought up than a barn." More yet. "You would not have lasted a day. Somebody would have had you in a pot within an hour. Why don't you stop wasting Aiden's time and figure out how you can help *the chosen one* save the town."

"Um... I don't think you understand. The delve belongs to our matchmaker. It proves helpful when arranging marriages when clarifying the... *status* of the individuals involved. Within hours of the dragon's announcement, everyone in Hardscrabble got together and made sure that no virgins remained."

"Well, at least the town got some pleasure out of the danger."

"What a terrible thing to say."

"Are you going to tell me you didn't help out the effort to thwart the dragon?"

Aiden blushed and stammered. "Well, of course… not that I did anything wrong. I helped save those girls' lives."

"Probably a few times, huh?"

"Well, we wanted to make sure… That's not the point. Because of what we all did, we had to look elsewhere. That's why I was sent off, but I might as well have been searching for the Dadga himself for all the luck I was having. I was sure I would find at least one maiden of virtue somewhere, but the delve told me there were none, except for children. I was toasting my failure when you walked in."

My eyes opened wide and I could feel my cheeks flush. Elon snickering echoed through the bar.

"Say what?" I whispered.

"My job wasn't to find a champion, the elders gave that to Garak. Since I was... responsible for making sure so many of our women were ineligible for the dragon's request, I was sent to find a replacement virgin."

"Dammit!" I felt my face flush as his words sunk in. I wasn't a chosen one, at least not in the sense I imagined. I was embarrassed by my foolishness, but soon I had another reason to be mortified.

Elon had fallen over onto the floor because she was laughing so hard.

'This is ridiculous."

Elon started to roll in hilarity and tables started to fall. I threw up my hands and walked outside.

Aiden chased me. "What did I say?"

"First off, I'm not a virgin," I whispered.

"Of course, you are. There is no shame in it and in this case, there's glory." With a wink, Aiden added, "When this is done,

I'll help you fix your condition."

First, I hit him, then I grabbed Aiden by his collar and lifted him off the ground. "I'll have you *fixed*. Are you calling me a liar?"

"No. It's just the delve is never wrong," said Aiden.

I threw the fey to the ground. "It is this time. Trust me."

"How could it be?"

He wasn't going away so I might as well get this over with. "A long time ago, I went through some changes."

"It happens to all girls when they become women," Aiden said.

I hit him again. He got smart and shut up. "Different changes. My body heals any wound I suffer and I don't seem to age anymore. One unfortunate side effect is that my body thinks the part of me that defines virginity is a wound and heals it."

"So then even though you've had sex, your maidenhood remains intact?"

"Repeatedly," I conceded. "Let me tell you, it takes some of the fun out of sex."

"That's wonderful."

"That's a matter of opinion."

"But if the delve cannot tell, I'll bet the dragon cannot either."

"Am I hearing you right? Are you asking me to commit suicide by sacrifice?" I demanded.

"Why wouldn't I? Better to sacrifice one so that many more can live," said Aiden.

"Not as far as the one is concerned."

"If you won't do it, just say so. I might still be able to find another virgin in time."

"With what? This?" I asked, holding up the delve. Aiden reached out, but I closed my fist and pulled it away. "I don't think so. Besides, how did you plan to get a woman to go along with this plan?”

“There are women who would volunteer.”

“I doubt it.”

“You’re wrong. Our mayor’s daughter, Marta, bravely offered herself.”

“Poor Marta’s not quite right in the head, is she?”

“Marta is bright, just noble. Unfortunately, the delve showed she did not qualify. I’m not sure which upset the mayor more – that revelation or the dragon’s demands.”

“So what did you plan to do if you found a virgin who said no?”

Aiden looked guiltily at the ground. “The elders gave me permission to bring a virgin back by any means necessary.”

“So you planned to kidnap one?”

Aiden’s eyes remained fixed on the ground. “Yes.”

“Why didn’t you try that with me?”

“Against a Daemor? I’ve heard what kind of warriors you are. I wouldn’t stand a chance.”

“That mean you weren’t going to try?”

“No. I still would,” admitted Aiden.

“You’re a real nice guy, Aiden,” I said, my voice polar.

Aiden’s head snapped up from the ground and he stared me in the eyes. “Everyone who means anything to me is going to die unless I do this! What would you do in my place?”

“If it were my granny, sisters, and brothers on the line, I honestly couldn’t say. But I wouldn’t sacrifice an innocent or throw my own life away,” I said.

“That’s a selfish attitude to take.”

“Really? I’m so glad to hear that. I know a mage who specializes in transformations. I’ll be happy to foot the bill to have you changed into a woman with pure maidenhood. If we leave now we can be there before dawn.”

“Really?” asked Aiden, ashen and worried.

“It’s for a good cause. We better hurry,” I said, moving

toward the stable. Aiden stood immobile. "What's the matter? You're going to save your town."

"I...I...I..."

"You're scared spitless," I said. Aiden nodded. "Then how can you ask someone else to do what you won't do yourself?"

"That's different."

"No, it's not. Neither was helping to deflower the girls of your town. You knew someone would have to go or you all would pay. Didn't matter as long as you got a little piece of the pie, did it?"

Aiden had tears streaking down his face. "You're right. If I fail, everyone I care about will be killed." Aiden wiped the moisture off his face and took a deep breath. "Take me to the mage."

I was impressed by his offer of self-sacrifice. Honestly, I didn't expect it, but it upped my opinion of Aiden.

"There may be another way."

"What do you mean?" Aiden said, relief practically oozing out of his pores.

"I already told you. Elon and I can take care of the dragon."

"A human and a small horse?"

I glared, barely stopping him before his foot was in his mouth up to the ankle. He put his hand up to block the blow he assumed was coming. I restrained myself just to keep him guessing.

"Could you really slay the beast?"

"Let's hope it doesn't come to that. I like to leave killing as a last resort."

It's not like these people had anyone to go to. Most of the rulers around here are next to useless. I learned while helping refugees during Thandau's reign that even if you wanted to move, the lands here in Faerie might not let you. These people might not have been able to run, so they coped, right or wrong.

When we walked back into the bar, I cringed. Elon was

up on top of one of the larger tables and getting down with her bad self. The mare was dancing and had somehow gotten Joer to join her. He was trying to get off the table, but Elon was faster and blocked him before he ever got near an edge. The young man was sweating bullets and those of his companions who had regained consciousness were laughing heartily at his expense.

"Oy. I warned him. I suppose I better rescue the poor guy."

"I'll wait here."

"Suit yourself," I said, moving toward the fjord. "Elon, c'mon down." The mare neighed. "No, I don't think he's interested, I think he's scared. His eyes are wide with fear, not desire." Elon turned to argue and that distraction was all the opening Joer needed. He bolted for the far end of the tavern and stayed there, with his back to the wall and a solid table in front of him.

"We'd better go," I suggested, but Elon was staggering over to Joer and his laughing buddies cleared a wide path. Elon was whinnying loudly.

Joer was terrified and cornered. "What's she saying?"

"She wants a goodnight kiss," I said. Joer sank to the floor, cowering under the table. Elon knocked the table aside with her muzzle and Joer's eyes appeared to be all pupils. My trusty mare was making kissy faces with her huge horse lips. It was not a pretty sight.

This was one of those times I wished Elon still wore a bridle. After tucking the delve between my bosoms, as Granny liked to say, I ended up wrapping both of my arms around her neck and pushing for all I was worth. It took several minutes, but I got her out the door.

Our camp was set up in a clearing in nearby woods. I still had the delve. I took it out and wrapped it up. I didn't need its light making me a target in the darkness, not to mention impairing my night vision. Fortunately, there was an almost full moon, which was literally blue tonight.

Old habits die hard. I used a lava heater instead of a campfire. The heat's as good, without the bright flames. Perfect for when you don't want to give away your position, but still don't want to freeze.

Fortunately, we weren't on a mission in hostile territory because Elon threw up on Aiden's boots then laid down and began snoring loudly. By default, that left me with first watch. What else was new?

Aiden used the time to tell me the rest of the details. The tribute was supposed to be delivered to the dragon on the first night of the full moon. Unfortunately for Aiden, he had not been careful when taking a faerie path and had lost several days in the process. He only realized his mistake when he glanced up at the night sky. The dragon was supposed to get his due tomorrow.

"It doesn't matter now. It's at least a five-day journey. I can only hope Garak found a champion."

"We'll leave in the morning and be in Hardscrabble by afternoon," I said.

"Kande, that's impossible," said Aiden.

"Not if we take faerie paths."

"But there are no safe paths near here," said Aiden. As a mystic realm, parts of Faerie folded over on other parts in seeming defiance of the laws of time and space. It allowed thousand-mile journeys to be covered in just a few steps or vice versa. Time could also warp, lengthening or shortening according to how the paths were traveled, a condition a bartender acquaintance of mine likes to call quantum geography.

Traveling the paths had inherent dangers. A wrong turn could get a wanderer hopelessly lost for an eternity, while a misstep could lead to death, madness, or things much worse. Safe paths were well traveled and generally held little danger, as long as the traveler stayed on the path to the next crossroad.

"I know my way around the paths."

"How? A map?"

"Mab always felt that a map was too dangerous if it fell into enemy hands." I pointed to my head. "It's all up here. Part of Daemor training. We never knew when we'd have to lead an assault or retreat quickly, so we were drilled on the paths constantly. I know the ones near here."

"If it means getting home in time, I'm willing to risk it." Aiken seemed to be mustering his nerve. He used his newly summoned courage to ask me something that had been on his mind. "Did I hear you mention Earth back there?"

"Yep. That's where I'm from. Brooklyn, New York."

"Come on, Earth is just a legend. Isn't it?"

"That's what folks back home would say about Faerie," I said.

"I would have guessed you were from Orun Rere. That seems to be where most of the dark-skinned humans are from."

"Orun Rere was founded by escaped slaves and some natives from my country. We do share a common ancestry and I've spent some time there learning about my history. We can all trace our roots back to a place called Africa. In fact, my mother gave me an African name."

"I thought your name meant a type of sweet."

"Not the way it's spelled. It means 'first born'. Elon's ancestry is from Norway. The fjords were used by Vikings and were stronger than much larger horses. They used mares because they tended to be more protective of their riders than stallions. I actually gave her an African name. Elon means 'gift of God' or 'God loves me'. Little did I know how much my trusty mare would buy into her own hype."

Elon's snoring paused a bit as if she were listening. Once she was no longer the topic of conversation, the snoring started back up again.

"So how did you end up here?"

"Because of Thandau, Mab had gone into exile on Earth. I met her there and came back with her when she staged her revolt."

"Why aren't you still with Queen Mab?"

"I served my time and I wanted a chance to explore the world I helped save. I'm still technically in the reserves."

"I've seen Daemor before. They weren't wearing the same armor you are."

"We have different armor." The only commonality was the badge which we equate with a uniform.

"Why wear something so revealing?"

In answer, I reached over with my sheathed sword and rested it under Aiden's chin. With a gentle movement, I realigned his gaze from my cleavage to my eyes. "Let's just say it can distract male opponents and, in battle, I'll take any advantage I can get." And the glamour part was none of his business.

"That makes sense," said Aiden, embarrassed at being caught. He had figured the moonlight hid where he was staring.

"You'd better try to get some sleep," I suggested.

"I'm not sure I'll be able to," said Aiden.

"Just close your eyes."

"But..."

"Try."

Aiden did and was surprised to find when he woke in the morning that it had worked.

We shared our rations with him. There wasn't time to hunt down anything fresh. It wasn't especially tasteful, but it was filling.

"Want some coffee?" I asked.

"What's that?"

"A taste of home. Try it."

Aiden did and if his face was any indication, he wasn't thrilled. "It's bitter."

"I guess it's an acquired taste. I know something that might help the taste. Yo, trusty mare, time to get up." Elon grumbled. She's never easy to get up in the morning, especially with a hangover. The only exception is under fire. Then she moved like greased lightning. "I need some milk." The mare sighed loudly but stood. I moved a collapsible bucket under the horse and reached out. Elon let loose a high-pitched whinny. "Sorry. Cold hands, warm heart."

Aiden stared. "Are you... milking her?"

"Sure. I got the idea from the Vikings. They used to make sure their war-mares were nursing so they had fresh milk when they traveled. Makes a nice change from rations. If you don't want it in your coffee, you could just drink it plain. With all she drank last night, you might even get a buzz off it."

"I haven't had milk since I was nursing at my mother's tit. I'll pass."

"Suit yourself." Elon moaned at the noise and Kande chuckled. The mare moaned louder. "Look, I'm sorry you're hung over, but it's your own fault. Want some coffee?"

The horse nodded. Aiden was nauseated as he watched me pour the coffee into another collapsible bucket, then add the mare's own milk to the drink. Elon noticed his discomfort, shrugged, and drank it. It wasn't a cappuccino, but it was better than water. The mare licked the bucket clean and I have to admit it did seem to help her mood.

We packed up the camp and we mounted Elon, although the mare might have had other preferences. The path was just a few minutes outside the village. Like port towns, villages popped up at a crossroad, where a faerie path folded back into traditional time and space. The paths rarely had the lights or mists one might expect. Usually, the locals simply put up a sign. Other faerie paths had no markings, which made them even more dangerous to travel. This one had several signs, one of them even in English.

"Does Elon know the way?"

"My trusty mare is also a Daemor. She went through the same training, wears the same emblem." Elon neighed. "Listen, you nag, you did not at any point outrank me."

"She really is a Daemor?"

"Mab doesn't discriminate against nonhumonoids. There are all kinds of Daemor. Including a dragon."

"How long until we get there?" asked Aiden. This path looked normal enough from within, so the only way to tell is when what can only be described as an off-ramp appears. As it happened, we were at our exit.

"About now," I said as Elon turned off.

The town square wasn't far. Aiden brought us to meet the town elders.

"Aiden, you did it! The bones be praised!"

"Actually, mayor, he completed Garak's quest. We're here to deal with the dragon," I said.

"Excuse me? You mean she's not... pure?" asked the mayor, dismayed. His line of vision was also lower than my face. At this point, he'd never have been able to pick me out of a line up if I was wearing a t-shirt.

"Well, actually Kande is..." Aiden's statement was cut short by my elbow slamming into his gut.

"My heart is pure so I have the strength of ten women."

"Really?"

"No, but we can handle a dragon. Elon and I are Daemor. We can take care of this little problem."

"Little? You know we're dealing with a dragon, not a zila lizard, right?" said the mayor.

"No, I wasn't paying attention. Thank goodness you were here to set me straight. I only brought my zila sword. I just can't handle a dragon without my dragon sword. We women just can't warrior without the right accessories," I answered.

The mayor's eyes lit up. "You really have a sword just for dragons?"

"Yeah, my caddie has it in my bag next to my nine iron," I answered.

"Where is this caddie? And how is he strong enough to handle iron?"

Sarcasm and cultural references flew over this guy's head. "I wouldn't be so impressed by someone just because they can handle iron." I unsheathed my sword and pulled the naked steel across my bare arm. It impressed the lot because if any of them had done it, they would have gotten burned. Fey and iron, even diluted in steel, mix about as well as humans and acid.

"Are you truly Daemor?" he asked.

"Do you know what the penalty is for imitating a Daemor?"

The mayor shook his head.

"Let's just say an impostor would never be able to do it again."

The mayor cupped his face in his hands and sighed. "There's been no word from Garak, so I suppose you are our only option."

"We could just leave if you like."

The mayor blanched and started waving his arms frantically. "No, no. It's just we never expected champions as illustrious as Daemor to come to our aide."

Elon lifted up her hooves to look as if she had stepped in something brown and smelly. I had to control a giggle. It would ruin my tough girl mystique. "Now about finances..."

The mayor nodded and sighed again as he put on a long face. "We are a poor village. We don't have much."

"That's what they all say, so I'll offer you a deal. We'll do it and take the delve as payment," I said. Elon whinnied in dismay. I whispered, "We can have it reprogrammed to find other things." Besides, the fact that it glowed when I touched it annoyed the hell out of me. "You know what one of these is worth?" Elon neighed and looked out the window at a horse who was very well endowed, even for a stallion. "No, absolutely not. I'm not pimping for you. You can handle your own love life." Elon grumbled softly but didn't argue. Turning my attention back to the mayor, I said, "That would be in addition to your hospitality in feeding us, restocking our supplies, and such."

"The matchmaker won't be happy, but it's a deal. Besides, after all the testing, we won't need it for another generation."

"Point us toward the dragon."

The cave where the dragon was rumored to be holed up was about two hours from Hardscrabble on foot. Elon covered the distance in less than thirty minutes.

I wasn't the best tracker, but I knew enough to get by. Something was wrong with the imprints on the surrounding hillside. "These aren't dragon footprints. They look like they were made by fake feet." Elon neighed. "You can't smell it? Could the scent be too old?" The mare shook her head. "What's going on here?"

I wasn't expecting an answer, but I got one anyway. A rather pathetic roar came forth from the cave, followed by a dragon that was anything but. The male dragon was tremendous, well-muscled and spat fire into the air. It was easily the second largest I had ever seen and it figures it had to be a fire dragon. I hate being burned. Yes, I heal, but I still feel the pain and go into shock like anyone else. The only difference is so far I've always survived, but I have nightmares for months. One of the other reasons I prefer lava heaters over campfires. No flashbacks.

My trusty mare suddenly lost her mind and charged at the great beast.

"Elon, no!" I screamed, but I was too late to do anything but watch as she continued her kamikaze assault.

My fear turned to confusion as Elon made contact with the dragon, running unharmed through a wall of flame to do it. Instead of being killed, she actually knocked down the dragon.

Which was impossible unless there was magic was in play and the magic wasn't coming from the horse.

Elon stormed toward the dragon again and it was on its back, scrambling away in actual fear. Her teeth chomped at its neck and she pulled. I heard metal snap and saw the flash of a chain. The scene before me changed instantly. A male fey lay where the dragon had been and the dragon had replaced Elon. It had a forepaw on the man's chest. The mare had seemingly vanished, but Faerie wasn't getting rid of Elon that easy.

It was a glamour amulet. I had drawn my sword by instinct when Elon had first attacked and it was still in my hand. I strolled up to the fey and I was smiling. The fey was screaming from the pressure of the limb resting on his rib cage. "You mind explaining why you're impersonating a dragon and extorting a town? Do you know what a real dragon would do to you if they found out?" It would be far worse than if Mab found a Daemor impersonator.

"Go away and give me back my amulet."

"I don't think so. Explain all this to me before I get testy."

"I don't have to tell you anything."

"Don't bet your life on it," I said. "Oh, wait, you just did. You can save yourself some pain if you came clean voluntarily. Wouldn't you agree, Elon?"

The horse disguised as dragon whinnied and nodded.

I waved my sword, then held it an inch from his nose. One touch and we'd be smelling barbequed fey. It wouldn't kill him, but it would hurt like hell.

A twig cracked behind us. Knowing Elon had the fey under control, I spun and drew my gun.

"Get away from Falin!" screeched a young fey girl, racing toward the man. She was unarmed so I didn't shoot her, however tempting it might have been. Her voice sound just like my kid cousin's whining when she used to follow me around when we were kids. "Are you okay, pumpkin?"

Just because she was unarmed, didn't mean I was going to let her have the run of the place. "Freeze. Who the hell are you?"

"Marta."

Elon and I shared a glance and smiled. Everything came together. Elon even smiled, which was terribly impressive on the dragon apparition just because of the size of the teeth alone. Elon stepped off and let the couple embrace.

"You're the mayor's daughter, who offered herself up to the dragon," I said just to let them know we had figured things out. "Why this scheme?"

"We just wanted to be together, what's wrong with that?" asked Falin. His whining wasn't as annoying as Marta's, but it just wasn't as becoming.

"In this case, lots. Why not just run away?"

"Well, we thought about it and we were going to and we even asked for permission to run away, but Daddy wouldn't let us. He said we were too irresponsible, too immature. He even had the nerve to say Falin was nothing but trouble," complained Marta, without stopping to take a breath.

She asked permission to run away? She was even worse than my cousin. "And this scheme proves him wrong how?"

"It was a good idea," said Falin.

"You're too modest, honey. It was brilliant. It would have worked too if they hadn't used the damn delve."

"Or if you hadn't been stupid enough to ask for something you knew you weren't."

"Falin was just supposed to ask for a maiden. It wasn't my fault he improvised the virgin bit."

"I figured it would get you in good with your father."

"Except now he knows I'm not. You can't imagine what he's been putting me through."

A crossbow bolt flew in and out of the dragon's illusionary head, embedding itself firmly in a tree.

"Down!" I ordered. This time my gun was already in my hand, so my bullet hit its target before I had finished talking. A hooded gentry found his crossbow shot from his grasp. "Looks like Garak completed his quest after all."

Elon and I sprinted toward the bowman. He dove for his crossbow, but the gunshot had ruined the firing mechanism. Seeing me and a "dragon" chasing after him, he realized he couldn't outrun us. Instead, he took a poisoned bolt in each hand and stood his ground. Gusty if I do say so myself. If Elon was a real dragon he had just tried to kill, he had no chance without the crossbow to deliver the poison. One burst of fire breath and he was a crispy critter, but he didn't run in fear.

We halted a safe distance away.

"The situation is under control," I said. "I don't need any assistance."

"I wasn't offering any. I was planning on killing the dragon. I'm not sure exactly what you were doing," said the gentry.

"There is no need to kill the dragon."

"I took a job and when Dogan takes a job, he finishes it. And I'm not giving up the reward."

"What reward? I thought the villagers didn't have much to offer."

"They don't. They promised me half of next year's crops. After I sell that, I'll be rich."

"Only if you live to collect it, which is definitely in question," I said. To accentuate my point, Elon tried to breathe fire, which the mare had deduced was actually caused by the person wearing the amulet spitting. Elon blew salvia out her lips horse style, which gave the flames the appearance of exploding fireworks, all without losing the amulet in her mouth. I raised an eyebrow in appreciation. "Also, half of the town's crops seems an awful lot like extortion to me, so I'm not sure I'd let you collect."

"I could cut you in for, say, ten percent."

"No thanks."

"Then step aside and let me kill it."

"No need." I waved my hand through the head of the dragon. "No dragon. A couple of kids with a glamour and a dumb idea."

"I'll just tell them I killed it."

"I think we'll tell them the truth. And a town that poor is probably planning on using the meat to help them through the winter to make up for the crops they traded you, so they'd insist on the corpse."

Dogan smiled. "Not to mention I'd have to kill the two of you."

I smiled back. It was so great having people in life or death situations looking so happy. It beat the usual screaming and name calling. "You shouldn't strive for the impossible. You'll just be disappointed. Besides we have you at a disadvantage, I mean you have only a pair of bolts."

"Perhaps, but consider yourselves lucky no one paid me to kill you, Kande," Dogan said, backing up toward nearby under and over brush.

"How do you know my name?"

"I am a professional."

"Meaning?" I asked. Dogan shrugged. "Don't feel too bad we got the drop on you."

"I don't and you didn't." Dogan slowly pulled his cape back to reveal wrist dart launchers. "These are rapid fire and I bet my clips hold more ammo than yours. Until we meet again." With that, Dogan stepped backwards until he disappeared. Unfortunately, he wasn't the only one.

"Marta and Falin are gone." Elon neighed. "No, it's not worth chasing them. I figure they're long gone." Elon whinnied again, posing in the dragon glamour. "I'd take it off," Elon responded. "No, I don't think you make an especially cute dragon and I don't think the stallion will either." The mare made a suggestion. "No, I won't pretend to be the dragon so you can save the stallion." Elon countered. "Yes, I'm sure he'd be grateful, but it would be deceitful. Have you ever thought about wooing him? Get him flowers or something." The mare answered. "Yes, I suppose he would only eat them, but would that be a bad thing? In the meantime, fork it over." I held out my hand and Elon spit the amulet into it. "Lovely, horse slime." Elon retorted. "No, a horse's mouth is not a hundred times cleaner than a human mouth. Especially not yours. After all, I know some of the places it's been."

I wrapped the amulet up and put it in a pack so the townspeople wouldn't think a dragon was attacking them when we returned. "C'mon, trusty mare. Let's go tell the mayor about his daughter and break his heart."

PATRICK THOMAS is the award-winning author of 40 books including the beloved fantasy humor Murphy's Lore series, which includes *Tales From Bulfinche's Pub, Fools' Day, Through The Drinking Glass, Shadow Of The Wolf, Redemption Road, Bartender Of The Gods, Nightcaps, Empty Graves, The Mug Life* — as well as the future space adventures *Startenders* and *Constellation Prize*.

The Murphy's Lore After Hours spin-offs star the half pixie/ogre Terrorbelle (*Fairy With A Gun, Fairy Rides The Lightning,* and *Terrorbelle The Unconquered*); the former demon-possessed serial killer Agent Karver of the Department of Mystic Affairs *(Dead To Rites, Rites of Passage)*; the cursed magí Hex *(By Darkness Cursed and By Invocation Only)*; Vince Argus, the Soul For Hire *(Greatest Hits)*; and Negral, a forgotten Sumerian god who works as Hell's Detective *(Lore & Dysorder, Bullets & Brimstone,* and the graphic novel *The Moon Maniac* with Blair Webb).

His Mystic Investigators paranormal mystery series includes *Shadows & Brimstone* (omnibus of *Bullets & Brimstone* and *From The Shadows* with John French), *Once Upon In Crime* (omnibus of *Once More Upon A Time* and *Parners In Crime* with Diane Raetz) *Mystic Investigators, Mean Streets,* and the upcoming *Fear To Tread. Assassins' Ball* is his first traditional mystery, co-written with John French. He co-edited *New Blood, Hear Them Roar, Camelot 13* and was an editor for the magazines *Fantastic Stories of the Imagination* and *Pirate Writings*.

His other works include the steampunk *As The Gears Turn* and the space epic *Exile & Entrance*.

Patrick's darkly humorous advice column Dear Cthulhu has been running since 2005 and includes the collections *Have A Dark Day, Good Advice For Bad People, Cthulhu Knows Best, Cthulhu Happens, Cthulhu Explains It All* and *What Would Cthulhu Do?* The Dear Cthulhu advice empire has expanded from magazines and books to radio as Dear Cthulhu now broadcasts monthly on the show *Destinies: The Voice of Science Fiction* which is hosted by Dr. Howard Margolin.

His short stories have been featured in over sixty anthologies and more than forty-five print magazines.

A number of his books were part of the props department of the CSI television show and *Nightcaps* was even thrown at a suspect's head. His urban fantasy Fairy With A Gun had been optioned for film and TV by Laurence Fishburne's Cinema Gypsy Productions. Top Men Productions has turned his Soul For Hire Story, *Act of Contrition*, into a short film.

He also writes books for kids as **Patrick T. Fibbs** including the *Undead Kid Diaries: Over My Dead Body*, the *Babe B. Bear Mysteries: Bad Hair Day* and the picture book *5 Silly Monsters Jumping On The Zed: A Ughabooz book* (all with artist Shawn Evans).

Please drop by www.patthomas.net or follow him at I_PatrickThomas at Twitter or www.facebook.com/PatrickThomasAuthor to learn more.

More GREAT Science Fiction!

THE STARSCAPE PROJECT
As his quest begins, an artificial intelligence li form enters the galaxy and launches a series covert attacks against the Empire. The Teconeans assume that the Federation is responsible, and galactic peace is about to unravel. As Stryker chases his nemesis into Teconean space, he finds himself thrown into middle of the battle. Knowing that Earth will be the aliens' next target, Stryker must decide whether to let them destroy the Empire, or to forces with his Teconean enemies against the invaders. The key to the mysterious aliens lie buried on the moon of Kennedy Prime, and it' up to Stryker to solve the puzzle before war begins. The fate of the galaxy is at stake.

ZONE OF THE TENTH DGREE
1912, an alien ship crash lands in the Atlantic ean, setting up a secret colony that remains detected for centuries, allowing them to nipulate some of the most important events in man history -- from the sinking of the Titanic to Bermuda triangle to global warming. Now, technology of the 26th century has covered the aliens' distress beacon, and it's a e against time as the Navy tries to stop a rorist armed with a nuclear weapon from stroying the colony and triggering an all-out r as the mother-ship approaches

Now available from
PADWOLF PUBLISHING

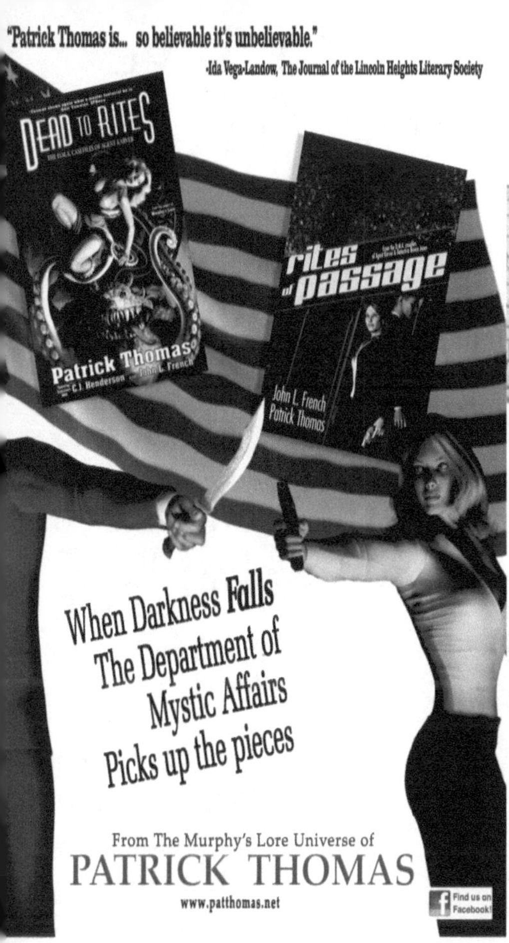
"Patrick Thomas is... so believable it's unbelievable."
-Ida Vega-Landow, The Journal of the Lincoln Heights Literary Society
DEAD TO RITES
Patrick Thomas
C.J. Henderson
John L. French
rites of passage
John L. French
Patrick Thomas
When Darkness Falls
The Department of
Mystic Affairs
Picks up the pieces
From The Murphy's Lore Universe of
PATRICK THOMAS
www.patthomas.net
Find us on Facebook!

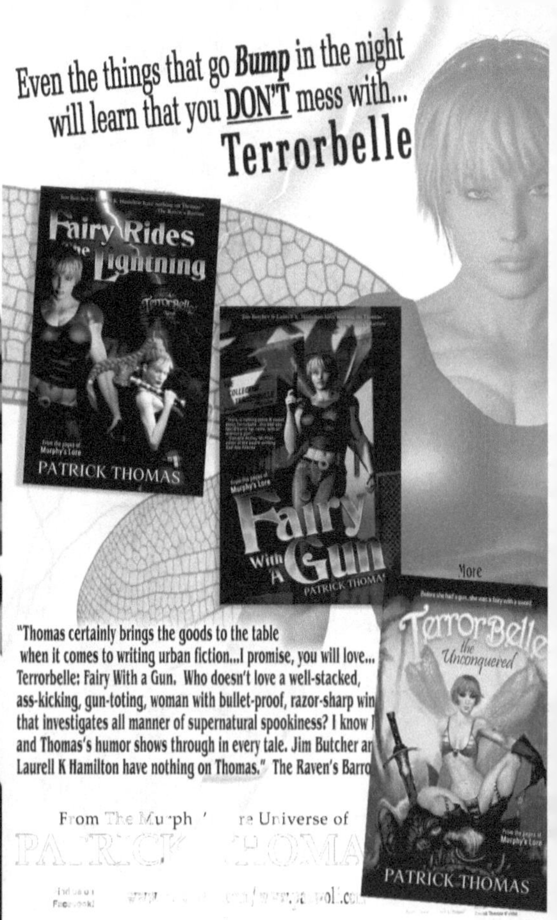
Even the things that go Bump in the night
will learn that you DON'T mess with...
Terrorbelle
Fairy Rides the Lightning
From the pages of Murphy's Lore
PATRICK THOMAS
Fairy With A Gun
PATRICK THOMAS
TerrorBelle the Unconquered
From the pages of Murphy's Lore
PATRICK THOMAS
"Thomas certainly brings the goods to the table
when it comes to writing urban fiction...I promise, you will love...
Terrorbelle: Fairy With a Gun. Who doesn't love a well-stacked,
ass-kicking, gun-toting, woman with bullet-proof, razor-sharp win
that investigates all manner of supernatural spookiness? I know I
and Thomas's humor shows through in every tale. Jim Butcher an
Laurell K Hamilton have nothing on Thomas." The Raven's Barro

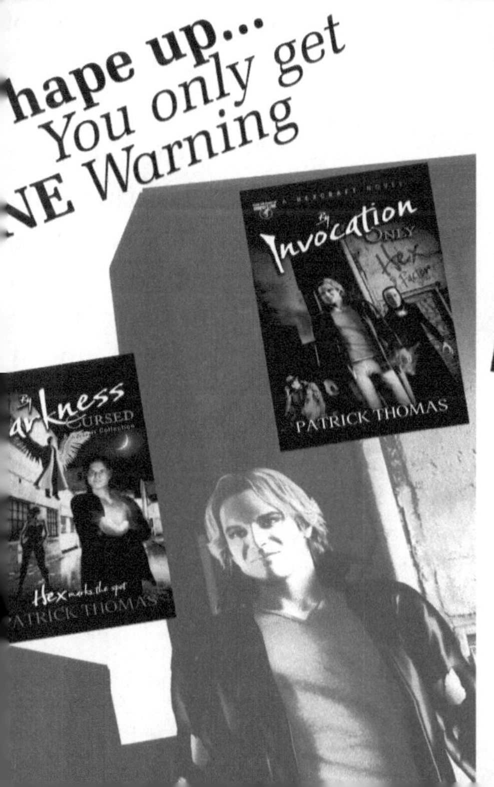
hape up...
You only get
NE Warning
By Invocation Only
PATRICK THOMAS
By Darkness Cursed
Hex marks the spot
PATRICK THOMAS

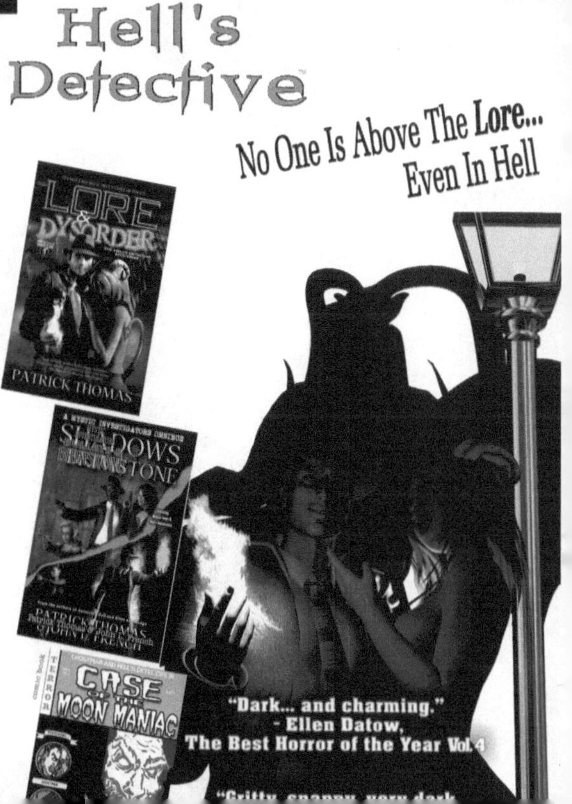
Hell's
Detective
No One Is Above The Lore...
Even In Hell
LORE & DYSORDER
PATRICK THOMAS
SHADOWS OF THE BRIMSTONE
PATRICK THOMAS
JOHN L. FRENCH
CASE OF THE MOON MANIAC
"Dark... and charming."
- Ellen Datow,
The Best Horror of the Year Vol. 4

One Last Chance to Save
Happily Ever After

Can a group of heroes including Goldenhair, Red Riding Hood and Rapunzel help General Snow White and her dwarven resistance fighters defeat the tyrannical Queen Cinderella? And will they succeed before a war with Wonderland destroys everything?

Their only hope to stop Cinderella's quest for power lies with a young girl named Patience Muffet who carries the fabled shards of Cinderella's glass slippers.

Roy Mauritsen's fantasy adventure fairy tale epic begins with *Shards Of The Glass Slipper: Queen Cinder.*

"Fantastic... A Magnificent Epic
-*Sarah Beth Durst* author
Into The Wild & Drink, Slay, Lov

"The Brothers Grimn meets Lord Of The Rings!"
-*Patrick Thomas,* author
of the *Murphy's Lore* series

"Shards is a dark, lush full-throttle fantasy epic that present a bold re-imagining of classic characters.
-David Wade, creator o
319 Dark Stree

"Roy Mauritsen's enchanting epic comes at a time when fairy tales are back in the forefront of our collective imagination."
-Darin Kennedy, short fiction author

PADWOLF
PUBLISHING

In paperback & e-boo
Find out more a
shardsoftheglassslipper.con
padwolf.cor

A detective's work is never done.
And don't call him Baby Bear . . .

15th Aniversary
Omnibus of
Books 1-6

The zombie
apocalypse
is over...

Now even undead kids have
to go to school

5 SILLY
MONSTERS
JUMPING ON
THE ZED

a picture book
for kids

www.talehaven.com

DOWN THESE MEANS STREETS
of Magic & Monsters walk the

MYSTIC INVESTIGATORS